A secret kiss . . .

"I'd rather be out here in the hall than in there," Aaron said. "It's pretty humiliating to stand alone by the refreshment table while your date dances with somebody else. I guess we're both in the same boat."

Elizabeth nodded dejectedly.

Aaron stood up. "Let's pretend we're each other's date for this last dance. That way we won't have to worry about what Todd and Jessica are doing." He held out his arms.

"OK." Elizabeth smiled. She put her arms around Aaron and they slow-danced to the romantic song coming from the gym.

"I really like this song," Aaron whispered. "Thanks for dancing with me."

Elizabeth looked up at Aaron. He was really sweet. And he was cute and charming, too. How could Jessica dump a great guy like Aaron to dance with Bruce Patman?

Suddenly Aaron's face was very close to hers. The next thing she knew, Aaron kissed her, very softly—right on the lips!

SWEET VALLEY TWINS titles, published by Bantam Books.
Ask your bookseller for titles you have missed:

SWEET VALLEY TWINS SUPER CHILLERS

SWEET VALLEY TWINS SUPER EDITIONS

SWEET VALLEY TWINS

The Great Boyfriend Switch

Written by
Jamie Suzanne

Created by
FRANCINE PASCAL

BANTAM BOOKS
TORONTO • NEW YORK • LONDON • SYDNEY • AUCKLAND

THE GREAT BOYFRIEND SWITCH
A BANTAM BOOK 0 553 40566 7

Originally published in U.S.A. by Bantam Skylark Books

First publication in Great Britain

PRINTING HISTORY
Bantam edition published 1993

Sweet Valley High and Sweet Valley Twins are registered trademarks of Francine Pascal.

Conceived by Francine Pascal.

Produced by Daniel Weiss Associates, Inc., 33 West 17th Street, New York, NY 10011

Bantam Books are published by Transworld Publishers Ltd., 61–63 Uxbridge Road, Ealing, London W5 5SA, in Australia by Transworld Publishers (Australia) Pty. Ltd., 15–25 Helles Avenue, Moorebank, NSW 2170, and in New Zealand by Transworld Publishers (N.Z.) Ltd., 3 William Pickering Drive, Albany, Auckland.

Printed and bound in Great Britain by Cox & Wyman Ltd., Reading, Berks.

The Great Boyfriend Switch

One

"It's going to be awful," Amy Sutton said.

"Amy!" Elizabeth and Jessica Wakefield exclaimed in unison.

"Well, it will be," Amy insisted, slamming the door to her locker shut. The three girls were standing in the hall of Sweet Valley Middle School before their first-period class.

"No, it won't," Elizabeth argued. "It's going to be fun. We've never had a school dance before. I think it's a great idea." Elizabeth's eyes sparkled with excitement. "Just think how nice the gym will look when it's all fixed up. I heard Mr. Sweeney is supervising the decorating." Mr. Sweeney was their art teacher and his class was one of Elizabeth's favorites.

"Forget the decorations," Jessica said with a wave of her hand. "I heard we're going to have a real DJ from Los Angeles."

"I can't wait!" Jessica and Elizabeth said in unison.

Then they laughed. It wasn't often that Elizabeth and Jessica Wakefield completely agreed on something—even though they were identical twins. Both girls looked the same on the outside, with their long blond hair and sparkling blue-green eyes. But on the inside, the two sixth graders were as different as night and day.

Jessica loved parties, boys, clothes, and gossip. She was a member of the Unicorn Club, which was made up of the prettiest and most popular girls at Sweet Valley Middle School. Her best friend after Elizabeth was Lila Fowler, another Unicorn, who was one of the richest girls in school.

Elizabeth thought the Unicorns were silly, and had secretly nicknamed them "The Snob Squad." Her own friends weren't necessarily the prettiest or the most popular girls in school, but Elizabeth thought they were more interesting and a lot more sensible than most of the Unicorns. Amy Sutton was her best friend after Jessica, and sometimes Amy could be a little *too* sensible.

"I don't care who the DJ is," Amy said, shaking her head. "I still say it'll be awful. What if the guys act like they do in the cafeteria? You know— throwing food and making disgusting noises."

"Todd wouldn't act like that," Elizabeth protested quickly. Elizabeth and Todd Wilkins had liked each other for a long time. Elizabeth liked to think of Todd as her sort-of boyfriend.

"Neither would Aaron," Jessica said. Aaron Dallas was *her* sort-of boyfriend. "Ken Matthews might, though," she added with a mischievous grin.

Amy frowned. "No, he wouldn't. Ken is way too mature."

The three girls looked at one another. Then they all started to laugh.

"Ken is waaaaaay too mature," Jessica mimicked.

"OK, OK." Amy blushed. "We all know who we like. Let's not tease each other about it." She shrugged. "I mean, they're all nice guys, but I just don't know how they're going to handle something like a dance."

Suddenly, the conversation was interrupted by the sounds of loud shouting and laughter coming from a row of lockers on the other side of the hall. Elizabeth looked over and saw Ken Matthews, Jerry McAllister, Todd Wilkins, Aaron Dallas, and Peter DeHaven horsing around.

Aaron was trying to shove Peter into one of the lockers, and the other boys were laughing as they tried to shut the door on him. "Cut it out," Peter exclaimed, laughing as loudly as the others as he struggled to escape from their grasp. "Seriously. Stop it!"

As the girls watched, Aaron and Ken tied the laces of Peter's sneakers together, then took the long ends of the laces and tucked them into the bottom locker. When they slammed the door shut, Peter was tethered to the locker. All the boys guffawed loudly.

"See what I mean?" Amy said under her breath. "Not exactly what you'd call *debonair*, are they?"

Elizabeth frowned. She had to admit that Amy had a point. When Elizabeth had imagined the dance, she'd pictured Todd and Aaron and Ken elegantly wending their way around the dance floor. Looking at them now, they looked anything but elegant.

"Talking about the dance?"

Elizabeth turned and saw Veronica Brooks, the new girl in school, giving her an unpleasant smile. Veronica was tall and pretty, with silky dark shoulder-length hair. Her family had just moved into the mansion next door to the Fowlers'.

"By the way, Elizabeth, congratulations on getting a ninety-eight on the math test yesterday," Veronica said. "I thought I was going to beat you, but I only got a ninety-seven. Are you always number one around Sweet Valley Middle School?"

"Not always," Elizabeth said, trying to smile. Elizabeth didn't usually have trouble getting along with people, but she was finding it difficult to like Veronica. Veronica had been acting so competitive and superior since she'd arrived in Sweet Valley that Elizabeth didn't quite know what to think.

Veronica threw a contemptuous look in the boys' direction. "At my old school, the guys didn't act like that. They were too cool." She said it loudly, obviously intending to be overheard, and Elizabeth noticed a few of the boys listening in. "We had boy-girl dances all the time," she continued. "I guess people are just more sophisticated there. The guys here are really pretty lame."

"What are you talking about?" Ken demanded, turning around to face them.

"We *are* having a dance and everything," Peter added.

Veronica gazed challengingly at the boys. "At my old school, we had *dates* to the dances."

Elizabeth almost laughed out loud at the look on the boys' faces. They had all done boy-girl things before—bike rides, bowling, parties, things like that. Jessica had even gone with Aaron and his parents to a couple of Lakers games.

But an actual *date* to an actual *dance* was different. Different and a lot more romantic.

Instead of responding to Veronica's challenge, the boys hurried off in different directions to their classes.

"Typical," Veronica said, rolling her eyes. "I really wish I could have stayed at my old school."

"So do we," Jessica muttered as Veronica walked away.

"Hi, Elizabeth," Todd said, walking up to Elizabeth's locker.

"Hi," Elizabeth said with a smile.

"Listen," Todd muttered, looking around nervously, "I, uh, was wondering . . ." He started scuffing his sneaker against the bottom of the locker. "Uh, you know, talking about this dance and everything, um, well, I was wondering if you wanted to go with me. You know, be my date?"

Elizabeth could hardly hide her surprise. "I'd love to," she answered shyly.

"Great!" Todd said, looking extremely relieved. "OK, so, uh, I'll see you later."

"See you later," Elizabeth replied.

As soon as Todd disappeared into a classroom Elizabeth hurried around the corner. She had only a few minutes before the bell rang, but she had to tell someone her big news. She spotted Amy standing at the end of the hall and rushed toward her.

"Guess what," she said breathlessly. "Todd just asked me to go to the dance with him."

"You're kidding!" Amy shrieked. "You mean like a real date?"

"A real date," Elizabeth confirmed.

At that moment, Veronica rounded the corner and headed toward them. Amy raised her eyebrows mischievously. "I've got to tell Veronica," she whispered. "Maybe this will make her feel better about being at Sweet Valley."

Veronica walked up to them. "What's with you two? Is the circus in town or something?"

"Well, Veronica," Amy said with a grin, "we just found out that the guys at Sweet Valley aren't as immature as you thought. Todd asked Elizabeth to be his date for the dance."

But Veronica didn't smile or congratulate Elizabeth. Instead she gave her a stony stare. "Number one again, huh, Elizabeth?" she said coldly. Then she turned on her heel and stalked off down the hall.

Amy and Elizabeth stared after her in surprise. "Wow," Elizabeth said. "She didn't look too happy, did she?"

By third period, Amy wasn't looking too happy, either.

"What's the matter?" Elizabeth asked as they walked to Amy's locker.

Amy sighed. "Jake Hamilton asked Lila Fowler to the dance. Aaron Dallas asked Jessica. Rick Hunter asked Tamara Chase. Patrick Morris asked Sophia Rizzo. She can't go, so he asked Nora Mercandy. And I've heard of about five other girls who have dates. This thing has really snowballed. Now I know how Veronica felt." Amy looked wistfully at

Ken Matthews, who was standing several yards away, shoving books into his locker.

Elizabeth followed Amy's look. "Maybe he's just too shy to ask you here at school."

"Hey, Amy," Ken called out, approaching them. "I wanted to ask you something."

"Yes?" Amy said eagerly.

"Would you—" Ken broke off, embarrassed. "Never mind."

"What?" Amy urged. "Would I what?"

Ken shook his head. "It's a bad idea."

"What's a bad idea?" Amy persisted.

Ken shrugged. "Would you mind if I borrowed your math book? I left mine at home this morning and I need to finish a few problems before seventh period."

Elizabeth saw Amy's face fall.

Ken must have noticed Amy's disappointed look, too. "It's OK if you don't want to lend it to me," he said quickly. "I understand. I don't like to lend books, either. I'll just ask Ms. Wyler if I can use hers during study hall."

Ken wandered off to his next class. Amy groaned as she watched him go. "Some girls have all the luck. And some don't have any. Guess which kind of girl I am."

"Come on, Amy. Don't feel bad," Elizabeth reassured her. "I bet hardly anyone will have a date for the dance."

* * *

Elizabeth couldn't have been more wrong. By lunchtime, dating fever had swept Sweet Valley Middle School.

As she walked into the cafeteria Elizabeth spotted Amy sitting with Melissa McCormick and hurried to join them. "Hi, you guys," she said.

"Hi, Elizabeth. Guess what?" Melissa said with a smile.

"You have a date for the dance?" Elizabeth guessed.

"Yep. Peter DeHaven."

Amy groaned sadly.

"Gee, thanks, Amy," Melissa said, laughing.

"It's not that I'm not happy for you guys," Amy explained. "But I'm feeling worse and worse."

As Elizabeth was about to respond she glanced up and saw Jessica rushing toward their table.

"Guess what," Jessica exclaimed breathlessly.

"Janet Howell broke a nail?" Amy said grumpily.

"Amy's not in a very good mood," Elizabeth explained.

Jessica sat down next to her sister. "Yeah, yeah, whatever. But listen, this will cheer you up, Amy. The Unicorns are having a special meeting this afternoon and it's going to be open to non-Unicorns. We'll be talking about the dance, and since so many of us have dates, the Unicorns thought it would be a good idea to have a fashion and beauty seminar. I mean, we *are* experts in that department."

Elizabeth raised her eyebrows in surprise. "The Unicorns are actually inviting non-Unicorns to a meeting? This *is* big news." She looked at her sister suspiciously. "Does Janet know about this?" Janet Howell was an eighth grader and president of the Unicorns. She was one of the most popular girls in the whole school, and normally she wouldn't be caught dead talking to any girl who wasn't a Unicorn.

"Believe it or not, this was Janet's idea. She's feeling generous because Denny Jacobson just asked her to the dance," Jessica said.

"Oh, great," Amy muttered. "Another one bites the dust."

"That's really nice of you guys," Elizabeth said, "but you know, Jess, I tried it once, and Unicorn meetings aren't exactly my—"

"We'll be there," Amy interrupted.

Elizabeth and Melissa turned to look at her in surprise.

"What time does it start?" Amy asked.

Jessica studied Amy a little suspiciously. "Four o'clock at Janet's," she said. "And listen, Amy. Don't try to make a joke out of it or this will be your first and *last* Unicorn meeting."

"Oh, no," Amy said sarcastically under her breath as Jessica got up and hurried away.

Elizabeth couldn't help giggling. "Amy, are you serious about this?"

"I need all the help I can get," Amy said. "Who knows, maybe I can pick up some advice on how to get a date."

"You don't need the Unicorns' help for that," Elizabeth said reassuringly.

"I have a feeling I do," Amy replied. "You know, it's a shame we were too busy solving mysteries to learn anything at that charm school we went to."

"What do you mean?" Melissa asked. "You guys were doing important stuff while everybody else was learning how to walk around with books on their heads."

Elizabeth smiled at the memory. She and Amy and their friend Maria Slater had stumbled onto a crime ring at the charm school they had attended. They had managed to figure out the mystery and expose the criminals.

"Yeah." Amy smiled. "But right now this fearless crime-stopper would rather have a date for the dance than a medal from the police department."

Two

"Quiet, please! Quiet!" Janet stood in the middle of her living room and clapped her hands. She was surrounded by a large, noisy group of girls, both Unicorns and non-Unicorns. "We have a lot of important matters to discuss. Can we please come to order?"

Finally the girls fell silent. Janet gave them her best club-president smile. "As you know, Saturday night will be a very special evening. I'm sure we're all going to want to look our best. Therefore, the first matter for discussion is, should I get my hair cut?"

Amy glanced at Elizabeth and rolled her eyes. "Who cares if Janet gets a haircut?" she whispered.

"I just want to know how I can get Ken to ask me to the dance."

"Shh." Jessica turned around and frowned.

Elizabeth and Amy didn't need to worry about being overheard, though, because the Unicorns had already launched into a spirited debate about Janet's hair.

"I say go really short," Kimberly Haver advised. "Short hair is so in."

"But Janet's got such a long face," Lila argued. Then she looked worried. "What I mean is, Janet has a very *oval* face. Longer hair is more becoming on a face like . . ."

"Like a horse," Amy said in a whisper.

"Shh!" Elizabeth hissed, trying not to smile.

". . . like Janet's," Lila finished.

The room buzzed with discussion until Janet clapped her hands again for quiet. "Let's have a vote," she said. "All those in favor of my getting a haircut, raise your hands."

About two thirds of the girls raised their hands. "All right, then." Janet smiled. "I'll get my hair cut tomorrow afternoon. Now, does anybody have any thoughts on the high heel question?"

"My mom told me I could get some, so I'm wearing them," Belinda Layton said. "I don't care what Mary says."

"But Belinda," Mary Wallace protested, "most of the guys are, well, not tall. Do you want to tower over them?"

"I don't care," said Belinda stubbornly. "I've been wanting high heels for ages, but my mom kept saying no. She said that when I was old enough to date, I'd be old enough for heels. This is my big chance and I'm taking it." Belinda threw Janet a challenging look, as if expecting an argument.

Janet shrugged. "Well, I'm sure that none of us would *dream* of telling each other what to wear. So go ahead, wear the heels."

She looked out over the room. "OK, let's talk about clothes. Mary, I think you should wear that really nice plaid miniskirt you have, with a red sweater. And Tamara, I think the lavender dress you wore to the charm school dinner would be perfect for the dance. Only don't wear it with those prissy pearl earrings. Wear big hoops or something."

"I thought they wouldn't dream of telling each other what to wear," Amy whispered to Elizabeth.

Elizabeth swallowed a laugh and tried to keep her face serious and interested-looking.

Mary nodded agreeably at Janet's suggestion. But Tamara scowled. "I've got a bright pink minidress I'd rather wear. Besides, those earrings are *not* prissy."

"But Tamara," Janet argued, "Kimberly's new outfit is bright pink, too. You don't want to be wearing the same color, do you? Besides, you're not a Summer person. Your skin is too green."

"Hey!" Tamara bristled. "What do you mean, my skin is green?"

There was an eruption of outraged argument.

"Her skin is totally green," Jessica exclaimed.

"There is no green in her skin. It's more bluish," Mandy Miller argued.

Grace Oliver shook her head. "Jessica's right. She's got the greenest skin I ever saw."

Tamara threw up her hands. "Well, what do you think, Belinda? What am I?"

"I'd say you're a Fall. Definitely a Fall," Belinda replied decisively.

"What are they talking about?" Elizabeth asked Amy.

"They're talking about their colors," Amy explained. "Some people are Winter, some are Summer, some are Spring, and some are Fall. It has to do with what tones are in your skin, and that's supposed to tell you what colors you should wear."

"Oh," Elizabeth said blankly. "Sounds kind of confusing."

Amy sighed impatiently and raised her hand.

"Amy," Janet said, pointing in her direction.

Amy stood up. "I know it's none of my business, since I'm not a Unicorn, but you guys should all go to Carnival, that clothing store in the mall. There's a big sign in the window that says they'll do a free color analysis for anybody who wants one. That way you can find out for sure whose skin is green and whose isn't."

The Unicorns burst into applause.

"Great idea," Lila said happily.

"Sounds like fun," Betsy Gordon called out.

Elizabeth gave Amy a curious look. "How did you know that?" she asked her quietly.

Amy blushed. "I went last week," she admitted. "And I'm a Winter."

Elizabeth stared at her, amazed. It was hard to imagine Amy doing something like that.

Amy blushed even deeper. "I was at the store anyway," she said defensively. "And I figured it couldn't hurt and it might help."

Janet called again for silence and gave Amy a smile. "That's a wonderful suggestion, Amy. It makes me realize what a good idea it was to open this meeting to nonmembers."

"*Now* maybe we can talk about something useful," Amy muttered to Elizabeth.

Janet held up a large clipboard. "I'd like to make a list of the names of each girl and her date, for the Unicorn archives. We'll include the non-Unicorns, too, for historical accuracy." She wrote her own name at the top and then Denny Jacobson's next to it. "Lila, your date is Jake Hamilton. Belinda, you're going with Jim Sturbridge. Mandy, your date is . . . who?"

"Peter Jeffries," Mandy volunteered.

One by one, Janet asked each girl the name of her date and added it to the list. Finally, she got to Amy.

"Amy, who is your date?"

"I don't have one," Amy replied.

Janet looked up, startled. There were sympathetic murmurs from the other girls.

"That's why I'm here," Amy said impatiently. "I was hoping you guys could help me."

Kimberly reached over and patted Amy on the shoulder. "You came to the right place."

"Amy?" Elizabeth asked. "Is that you?"

It was the next morning at school, and Elizabeth was pretty sure she had spotted Amy in the hall. But this Amy had eyelids that were purple and blue, with thick eyeliner smudged around the edges.

"What do you think?" Amy asked. "Lila and Kimberly did it this morning before school. They decided I needed a makeover. It's supposed to make me look glamorous."

"Well," Elizabeth said uncertainly, "it certainly is a *different* look for you."

"But will it make Ken notice me?"

"You'll find out in about two seconds, because here he comes now," Elizabeth said in a low voice. The two girls paused outside their English class and watched Ken come down the hall in their direction.

As soon as he saw Amy's face his eyes widened and his jaw dropped. "Wow," he said, staring at her eyes. "What does the other guy look like?"

Elizabeth had to bite her lip to keep from laughing. Amy really did look as though she'd been punched in both eyes.

"Does it hurt much?" Ken asked, his face concerned.

"No," Amy said through clenched teeth.

Ken gave Amy a sympathetic pat on the shoulder. "I know it's hard to do, but next time just walk away. Fighting never solves anything." He gave Amy's arm a friendly squeeze and headed down the hall.

Elizabeth could see Amy's embarrassed flush even under the thick coat of powder covering her face.

Amy threw up her arms in frustration. "Now what?"

Elizabeth smiled. "Well, at least he noticed you."

*   *   *

"Congratulations, Elizabeth," Mr. Bowman said. "I finally finished grading the essays I assigned a couple of weeks ago. Your grade was the highest in the class."

The English teacher smiled at Elizabeth as he put her paper down on her desk. Elizabeth grinned.

"Way to go," Todd mouthed.

Amy smiled at Elizabeth, too. Her eyes sparkled behind her thick eye makeup.

Mr. Bowman held up a second essay. "Veronica, congratulations to you, too. It was a very good effort. A little more work and you'll be giving Elizabeth some serious competition."

There was another burst of applause, but Elizabeth noticed that it was much less enthusiastic. She turned to congratulate Veronica. But Veronica was looking at her through narrowed eyes, and her expression was so resentful that Elizabeth changed her mind.

After class, Todd came over and gave Elizabeth a shy smile. "Congratulations on that essay. You're a really good writer."

Strangely enough, Elizabeth felt shy, too. She talked to Todd all the time. They'd known each other since kindergarten, and she'd always liked him because he was so smart and nice and easy to talk to. But now, with the prospect of a date looming over them, things seemed to have changed. Todd was looking a lot older all of a sudden. He looked really cute, too. Elizabeth's heart began to beat a little faster than usual.

"Well," Todd said, "I'll see you later."

"See you," Elizabeth said, smiling after him.

Amy grabbed her elbow. "Let's stop in the bathroom. I want to wash this goo off my eyes."

Elizabeth turned to examine Amy's eye makeup as they walked along. "Good idea," she said. "I don't think it's really you. Anyway, you shouldn't worry. I think Ken will—yikes!" Elizabeth broke off as she bumped right into Veronica, who was also on her way into the bathroom.

"Do you *mind*?" Veronica asked in a nasty tone. "You just stepped right in front of me."

"I'm sorry," Elizabeth said. "I was so busy talking to Amy that I didn't see you."

"I know you're used to being first in everything," Veronica sneered. "But this time you'll just have to be second." She pushed right past Elizabeth and went into the rest room.

"Wow," Amy said as the door swung shut in their faces. "Come on, let's go to the other bathroom. She looks mad enough to bite."

Elizabeth shook her head in bewilderment. "What's she so mad at me about?"

"Maybe it's because you keep beating her at everything," Amy said thoughtfully. "It seems to me as if she's one of those people who is always trying to be better than everybody else. The only person she can't seem to beat is you. She gets a ninety-seven on the math test. You get a ninety-eight. You get the best grade on your English essay. She gets the second-best grade. And I have a feeling I know what's bugging her the most—that Todd asked you to the dance instead of her."

Elizabeth's eyes widened.

"Seriously. Kimberly told me this morning that the first day Veronica was here she asked her who Todd was. She said she thought he was the cutest guy in the sixth grade."

"Oh, boy," Elizabeth said, shaking her head.

"You know," Amy added, "I'll bet she brought

up that dating stuff hoping that he'd ask her. But he didn't. Nobody did." Amy sighed unhappily. "It looks like Veronica and I are the only two girls who won't have dates for the dance."

"Amy! Amy! Wait up!"

Elizabeth and Amy turned and saw Ken hurrying toward them.

"He probably wants to borrow my history notes," Amy muttered.

Elizabeth giggled. "Don't be so negative. And *smile*."

"Hi, Ken," Amy said with a big smile as he caught up with them. "What's up?"

Ken looked up and down the hall. "Have you noticed what's going on around here?" he asked, sounding disgusted.

"I'm not sure," Amy answered. "What are you talking about?"

"I'm talking about this dating stuff. I can't believe how silly everybody's acting, can you? We're the only two people who aren't acting totally ridiculous. I don't want to get roped into it, and I figured you wouldn't either. So maybe we'd better plan on sticking together at the dance."

Amy's mouth fell open in surprise.

Ken appeared to be thinking hard. "As a matter of fact, just to be on the safe side, we probably should plan on going together."

Amy shook her head, looking bewildered. "But Ken, wouldn't that be like—well—a *date*?"

Ken gave an embarrassed snort. "Of course not. Don't be so lame, Amy. So what do you say? Want to go together?"

Amy shrugged, trying to keep her voice casual. "Sure, I guess so."

"Great," Ken said, sounding relieved.

He walked off and Amy gazed after him. Then she turned to Elizabeth and they both started to laugh.

"All right, Amy!" Elizabeth exclaimed. "You did it. You've got a date."

Amy snorted in a pretty good imitation of Ken. "Don't be so lame, Elizabeth. It's not a date. We're just going to the dance together. And sticking together when we get there. And leaving together." She rolled her eyes and shook her head. "Give me a break!"

"Why don't you come over to my house to get ready before the dance?" Elizabeth suggested. "It'll be fun to get dressed together. I'll see if Melissa wants to come, too." She frowned in mock concern. "You don't think that's too lame, do you?"

Amy pretended to think it over. "Yeah, it probably is. But what the heck. I'm beginning to suspect that underneath these sensible exteriors, we're pretty lame after all."

Three

◇

"Has anybody seen my brush?" Lila shrieked from the bathroom that connected Jessica's and Elizabeth's bedrooms.

"It's horrible," Janet wailed. "Just horrible." She poked her head into Elizabeth's room. "Look at this," she said in a tragic voice. "It's hopeless." The top of her new shorter hairdo was standing straight up. "What am I going to do?" But before anybody could answer, she had disappeared back into the bathroom.

"I need some lipstick," Mandy's voice rang out.

It was the night of the dance, and the Wakefield home was pandemonium. Several of the Unicorns had come over to dress in Jessica's room.

Amy and Melissa had come over to dress in Elizabeth's room.

The bathroom was filled to capacity with girls trying to put on makeup and fix their hair. "This is what I imagine a dormitory's like on Saturday night," Elizabeth said with a giggle as she shut the door between her room and the bathroom.

"This is fun," Melissa said, pulling on her leggings. "I was afraid my first date would be really nerve-wracking. But there's too much going on to get nervous."

Elizabeth opened the closet and pulled out a pink minidress with a patent-leather belt. "What do you think?"

"It's gorgeous." Amy sighed as she pulled on her denim miniskirt. "I should have gotten something fancier to wear."

"But that looks great on you," Elizabeth protested. She watched Amy button up the crisp white shirt that went with the skirt. "I like tailored clothes. I think they look more sophisticated than frilly dresses."

"Do you really think so?" Amy asked hopefully.

"Definitely," Melissa and Elizabeth answered together. Then all three girls started laughing.

"We're beginning to sound like the Unicorns," Amy said with a chuckle.

The door opened and Lila and Kimberly came hurrying in. "Let's see how you look, Amy." Kimberly briskly inspected her. "Hmm. Maybe we should put some eye makeup on you."

"No!" Elizabeth, Amy, and Melissa cried in unison.

"We're just trying to help," Lila said huffily.

"Thanks," Amy said quickly. "And I really appreciate it. But the eye makeup didn't get the kind of response from Ken that I was hoping for."

Lila tapped her foot and looked thoughtful. "What you need is a scarf," she said decisively. "Your outfit is a little severe. Wait here."

Before Amy could respond, Lila had whisked into the bathroom and returned with a beautiful silk scarf. "Here. Wear this," she said, draping it around Amy's neck.

Elizabeth couldn't believe how friendly the Unicorns were being. Kimberly and Lila were being especially nice to Amy. They seemed to regard her as their own personal project.

Amy fingered the scarf. "It's really pretty, Lila. But don't you want to wear it?"

"Oh, I've got a couple more scarves in my purse," Lila said. "Don't worry about it. If you like it, you can keep it." Even though Lila probably had the biggest and most expensive wardrobe of any girl at Sweet Valley Middle School, she wasn't usually very generous about sharing it.

"Oh, I couldn't do that." Amy darted an amazed look at Elizabeth. "But if you think it looks good, I'll borrow it for tonight."

"Whatever," Lila said.

Kimberly frowned at Amy. "She needs something else. But what?"

Kimberly and Lila looked at each other, and then seemed to be struck by the same idea. "Heels!" they said in unison.

They hurried into the bathroom. "Belinda," Elizabeth heard Kimberly shout. "Can Amy wear your other shoes?"

A few seconds later, they came hurrying back with a pair of navy pumps. "Put these on," Kimberly ordered.

"These will really make Ken sit up and pay attention," Lila assured her.

Amy gingerly stepped into the high heels and walked around the room with her ankles wobbling.

"They'll really make Ken *stand* up and pay attention, too," Melissa whispered to Elizabeth. "Amy's at least as tall as Ken even when she's barefoot."

"You're right," Elizabeth said. She tried to think of a tactful way to tell Amy that the high heels might not be such a good idea. She didn't need to worry, though. The next thing she knew, Amy was plunging headfirst across the room.

"Help!" Amy shouted, plowing into Kimberly and Lila like somebody on runaway roller skates. They each grabbed her by an arm and steadied her.

"I think maybe I'd better stick to flats," Amy said sheepishly.

"Don't worry," Kimberly said with a grin. "Belinda isn't having much luck with them, either."

"Yeow!" they heard Belinda yelp from Jessica's room.

"See what I mean?" Kimberly said.

Amy took off the shoes and handed them back to Kimberly. "Thanks, but I think I'll just stick with the scarf."

"No problem," Kimberly said. Then she and Lila hurried back through the bathroom into Jessica's room.

Elizabeth, Amy, and Melissa began to laugh. "Does it seem like the Unicorns are being unusually nice?" Elizabeth asked.

"Yes. It's downright eerie," Amy said. "There must be something in the water making everybody act weird."

"I don't know about the water, but there's romance in the air," Melissa said. "I guess when you're feeling romantic, it makes the whole world rosy, and you feel like being nice to everybody."

"You're right," Elizabeth admitted with a blush. "We *are* all feeling romantic. I know I am. Isn't that silly?"

"It sure is," Amy said. "After all, it's the same bunch of guys we've seen every day since the first grade."

Elizabeth laughed and zipped up her dress. "Do you think the guys are feeling this way, too?"

Before Amy could answer, they heard Mr. Wakefield yelling in the hallway.

"Evacuate immediately. This is an emergency. Please head for the nearest exit. Those needing medical treatment will be seen on the patio."

"What's going on?" Melissa asked breathlessly. They all ran to the bedroom door and saw Mr. Wakefield standing in the hall. He was staring into Jessica's room with a horrified expression on his face.

"Dad!" Jessica wailed in an embarrassed voice as the Unicorns crowded out of her room into the hall. "Please!"

"What's the emergency, Mr. Wakefield?" Amy asked.

"I don't know," Mr. Wakefield replied, shaking his head grimly. "Looks like it was an avalanche. Or maybe a tornado. Hard to say. Could have been an earthquake."

Elizabeth, Amy, and Melissa walked down the hall and peered into Jessica's room. They all began to laugh. It really did look like a disaster area. There were clothes everywhere. Chairs were turned over. The floor was littered with hair ornaments and makeup cases. Blow dryers and curling irons were plugged into every outlet. And the mirror was covered with smears of makeup.

Just then, the twins' fourteen-year-old brother, Steven, came ambling out of his room. When he saw the crowd of girls and the state of Jessica's room, he froze.

"Don't worry about us," Mr. Wakefield commanded. "Save yourself—if you can."

Steven quickly ducked back into his room and shut the door with a loud bang. "Call me when it's over," they heard him shout from the other side of the door. All the girls burst into laughter.

"Coward!" Mr. Wakefield teased him through the door. "High school freshmen were made of sterner stuff in my day." Then he smiled at the group. "You all look very pretty," he said. "Come downstairs and I'll take a picture."

The girls headed down the stairs, laughing and chattering and making last-minute adjustments to their hair and clothes. Mrs. Wakefield stood at the bottom, clapping her hands. "You're gorgeous! All of you!" she exclaimed.

The girls quickly arranged themselves on the steps for a group picture. Jessica and Elizabeth sat together in the front and put their arms around each other.

"Everybody say *boys*," Kimberly said with a giggle.

"*Boys!*" the group shouted as Mr. Wakefield snapped the picture.

A second later the doorbell rang, and a sudden hush fell over the room. The girls stood up and looked at one another nervously. The big moment was finally here. Somebody's date had arrived.

Mr. Wakefield cleared his throat and walked to the door. As he swung it open every girl drew in her breath.

"Good evening," Mr. Wakefield said in his deepest and most formal voice. "Won't you come in?" He stepped back and bowed in an elaborate gesture of welcome, sweeping his arm in a wide circle.

"He is sooooo embarrassing," Jessica moaned. Elizabeth and Amy laughed.

Peter Jeffries and Peter DeHaven stepped through the door, looking nervous. They were dressed in sport coats and neatly knotted ties. "Good evening, sir," they said in unison.

Melissa and Mandy smiled shyly at their dates and hurried to get their purses. "My dad is driving," Peter DeHaven explained to Mr. Wakefield.

"Don't do anything I wouldn't do," Mr. Wakefield said with a wink as the girls returned and the foursome headed out the door.

Elizabeth saw her mother elbow her father in the ribs. "Have a wonderful time," Mrs. Wakefield told the departing couples with a smile.

Amy and Elizabeth sat down side by side on the bottom step. "I hope Ken doesn't show up until last," Amy said. "It's fun watching everybody else leave."

Elizabeth smiled. "I know. Can you believe how mature the boys are acting?"

"No," Amy said. "It's amazing. I guess I was

wrong about them not being mature enough for a dance." She shrugged and sighed happily. "I think tonight might actually turn out to be fun."

"I know it will be," Elizabeth said confidently.

The doorbell rang again, and Elizabeth couldn't help blushing when Todd and Aaron stepped inside. Elizabeth knew that she looked especially nice that evening, and the look on Todd's face showed that he noticed. "Hi, Elizabeth," he said, swallowing nervously.

"You look great," Aaron said, grinning at Jessica. "This is going to be a fun night." He moonwalked across the front hall, making everybody laugh. "I'm ready to dance. Let's *go!*" he shouted.

"We're going, we're going," Jessica exclaimed with equal enthusiasm.

Elizabeth exchanged amused glances with Amy. Aaron and Todd were so different. Todd was quiet and thoughtful. Aaron was silly and outgoing. But each boy was nice in his own way. It reminded Elizabeth of the difference between herself and Jessica.

The two couples started out the door. Suddenly Jessica stopped. "Hold it! I forgot my purse." She turned and raced up the stairs. "Does anybody remember where I put it?" she shouted.

Elizabeth sighed, thinking of the state of Jessica's room. "It'll take her forever to find it."

"That's OK," Todd said quickly. He took

Elizabeth's hand and pulled her out the front door. "I want to talk to you for a minute in private, anyway." Then he just stood there for a minute, looking around uncertainly.

"Is something wrong?" Elizabeth asked, confused.

"I just wanted to make sure we're alone," he said. He reached into his pocket and handed her a little gold box. "This is for you."

"Todd! You didn't have to bring me a present."

"I know. But I wanted to give you something so you would always remember our first dance."

Elizabeth opened the little box. Inside was a little gold heart-shaped locket. "It's beautiful!" she gasped.

Todd took the locket and opened it. "See, I put our pictures in it."

Elizabeth saw that Todd had put a picture of himself on one side of the locket and a picture of her on the other side. It was so romantic that she didn't know what to say.

"Do you like it?" he asked hopefully.

"I love it," she replied sincerely. "It's so beautiful. Help me put it on."

Just as Todd finished fastening the locket around Elizabeth's neck, Aaron and Jessica came rushing out the front door.

"Sorry about the delay," Jessica said.

Elizabeth smiled at Todd. "No problem."

"Let's go," Aaron said excitedly. He grabbed Jessica's arm and propelled her toward his father's car, which was waiting for them at the curb. "Get ready to have the best time anybody's ever had in the Sweet Valley Middle School gym!"

Four

◇

Jessica stood by the punch bowl, her shoulders moving to the music. So far, the evening had been absolutely perfect. She and Aaron had been dancing nonstop since they arrived. The gym looked beautiful—colorful crepe paper hung from the ceiling, and the lights were dim and romantic.

Suddenly Elizabeth appeared at her elbow. "Where's Aaron?" she asked, helping herself to a glass of punch.

"He and a couple of the guys went over to talk to the DJ and make some requests," Jessica said. "Where's Todd?"

"He's talking to Amy and Ken," Elizabeth replied. "He'll be over in a minute. This is really fun, isn't it?"

As Jessica nodded enthusiastically she noticed Bruce Patman looking at her from across the room. It was the fourth time she had caught him staring at her. She couldn't help remembering that he had asked her to save him a dance before the dance marathon the Unicorns had held recently. He hadn't shown up for the actual event, but still, Jessica wondered if it was possible that he liked her. All of the Unicorns considered Bruce the cutest seventh grader in the whole school. He was also one of the richest—his family had as much money as Lila's. Some people thought Bruce was conceited, and Jessica had to admit that he was, kind of. But she figured he had a lot to be conceited about. She flashed another look in his direction.

"So, Jessica, who are you making eyes at now?"

Jessica turned and saw Rick Hunter at the punch bowl. "Is it my imagination, or are you staring at Bruce Patman?" he teased.

Jessica felt her cheeks burn. Rick Hunter was a cute and popular seventh grader. Jessica had always thought he was nice, but lately it seemed as though he never missed an opportunity to needle her. "You've got it backwards," she said frostily. "Bruce has been staring at *me*."

Rick grinned and exchanged a knowing look with Elizabeth. "Well, excuuuse me," he said with a laugh. He grabbed two glasses of punch and headed back toward Tamara Chase, his date.

"What does he know?" Jessica muttered as she watched him leave. Then she smiled and nudged Elizabeth. "Bruce is looking this way again. Do I have enough lip gloss on? How's my hair?"

Elizabeth rolled her eyes. Jessica wasn't exactly known for her modesty. But when Elizabeth looked up, she saw that this time Jessica wasn't just bragging. Bruce Patman *was* coming toward her.

Bruce stopped in front of the twins and gave Jessica an approving smile. "Hi, Jessica. Looking good. Want to dance?"

"Sure," Jessica said quickly, pretending not to see Aaron coming toward her from the DJ's booth. *Aaron is really cute and everything*, she thought, *but he's no Bruce Patman.*

As she started to follow Bruce to the dance floor she felt an insistent tug on her sleeve. "What about Aaron?" Elizabeth whispered.

Jessica shook off Elizabeth's hand. "It's just one dance," she whispered back. "Aaron won't mind." She hurried to catch up with Bruce on the dance floor. She was sure she saw several girls throwing her envious looks as she and Bruce started to dance.

Bruce looked even cuter than usual that night. He was a good dancer, too. Most of the middle-school guys looked kind of clumsy and weird when they tried to dance, but Bruce looked really cool. Jessica knew that she was a good dancer, too, and she was sure that together they made a terrific-looking couple. She hoped the other Unicorns were watching.

When the dance was over, Bruce smiled down at her. "Want to stick around for another one?" he asked.

"Sure," Jessica said with a big smile, tossing her head to the beat of the next song.

"Is Jessica going to dance with Bruce Patman all night?" Todd asked. "I thought she was Aaron's date."

As Todd twirled Elizabeth around she caught a glimpse of Aaron standing by himself at the refreshment table. She watched as he poured himself another glass of punch and stared glumly at Jessica and Bruce.

"She *is* Aaron's date." Elizabeth sighed. "But I guess she'd rather dance with Bruce."

"What's so great about Bruce, anyway?" Todd asked. "Why do all the girls act so ridiculous when he's around?"

Elizabeth laughed. "I don't know. He's cute, but he's not very nice. I've heard him say things that really hurt people's feelings."

"He seems like a real jerk to me. Maybe girls just like guys who are jerks," Todd said philosophically.

Elizabeth glanced down at her locket. "Not all girls." She smiled up at him. "I prefer guys who are nice and considerate. I can't imagine you hurting anybody's feelings. That's one of the things I like most about you."

Todd smiled back at her. "What a coincidence. That's one of the things I like most about you, too."

Elizabeth saw that he was blushing, and she knew that she was blushing, too. They were beginning to sound pretty mushy. "Let's go keep Aaron company," she said quickly. "He looks like he could use it."

Todd and Elizabeth left the dance floor and walked over to the punch bowl. "How's it going, Aaron?" Todd asked, trying to sound cheerful.

But Aaron didn't smile. "OK," he said gloomily.

Todd and Elizabeth exchanged worried glances. "How's the punch?" Elizabeth asked.

"I don't know. I've had so much of it, I can't even taste it anymore," Aaron muttered.

"At my old school, they served cappuccino with ice cream at the dances." Aaron, Elizabeth, and Todd all turned and saw Veronica Brooks wrinkling her nose at the purple punch. "That looks like Kool-Aid or something."

"It's not so bad," Todd said. "Here, try some." He poured out a cup for Veronica and handed it to her.

But Veronica put it on the table untouched. "I'd rather dance than drink punch," she said. "How about it, Todd?"

"Well," Todd stammered, "I'd love to, but . . ."

Veronica took a step closer to him. "You wouldn't want to hurt my feelings, would you?" she said.

"Uh, no," Todd replied, looking genuinely troubled. He threw an apologetic glance in Elizabeth's direction, then took Veronica's arm. "We'll be right back," he said to Elizabeth and Aaron.

She's sure got a lot of nerve, Elizabeth thought, annoyed. *Why didn't Todd just tell her no?* But then she sighed. She couldn't get too angry. Hadn't she just told Todd that one of the things she liked most about him was that he was so kind and considerate? Elizabeth knew that he would never intentionally hurt anybody's feelings.

Aaron patted her shoulder sympathetically. "Looks like we both got dumped," he said sadly.

"Todd will be back soon," Elizabeth said quickly. She glanced over at Aaron. "And so will Jessica," she added softly, hoping that it was true.

Four songs later, Elizabeth wondered if her face looked as glum as Aaron's. *How nice does Todd have to be?* she wondered angrily.

During the first two songs, Todd had given Elizabeth a couple of apologetic looks. But somewhere around the third song, he had stopped looking over at her. Instead, he'd started smiling and laughing with Veronica. The fourth song was a slow number, and when it started Veronica had wrapped her arms around Todd and begun to sway to the music. Todd hadn't put up any resistance at all, as far as Elizabeth could see.

On the other side of the room she could see Bruce and Jessica dancing. There was a bright spotlight hanging right above them. Sometimes they stepped into the beam and were visible, and other times they stepped out of it and were hidden in darkness.

Aaron put down his cup of punch with a bang. "I've had enough of this. I'm cutting in on Bruce," he said angrily. "Jessica's supposed to be my date and this is the last dance."

At that moment, Elizabeth saw Bruce and Jessica step into the light. Elizabeth had a perfect view of Jessica's face as she gazed up at Bruce adoringly —and she had a perfect view as Bruce slowly bent down and gave Jessica a long, lingering kiss!

Elizabeth drew in her breath with a gasp. She heard Aaron gasp, too, just before he turned and stalked away.

"Wait!" Elizabeth cried, running after him. She felt terrible for Aaron. How could Jessica do this to him?

She followed Aaron out of the gym into the hallway. "Don't feel bad," Elizabeth begged. "You know how Jessica is. She doesn't mean anything by it."

"All I know is that Jessica is supposed to be my

date and she dumped me," Aaron said bitterly.
"Not only did she dump me, she's kissing some
other guy in front of the whole school! What's with
her, anyway? I'd never treat a date like that. Neither would you, I bet. Nobody would. Nobody except Jessica."

That made Elizabeth think of Todd, and she
began to feel sorry for herself as well as for Aaron.
She had thought Todd would never treat her that
way, either. But he certainly seemed to be having a
good time dancing with Veronica.

Aaron put his hand on Elizabeth's arm. "I'm
sorry. I know you've got troubles of your own.
Don't worry about Todd. I'm sure he'll be back any
minute. Why don't you go back inside?"

"I don't want to go back inside," Elizabeth said
quickly. She really didn't. It was too embarrassing.

Aaron nodded sympathetically. "I know how
you feel. I'd rather be out here than in there. It's
pretty humiliating to have everybody see you
standing alone by the refreshment table while your
date dances with somebody else. I guess we're both
in the same boat."

Elizabeth was surprised to hear Aaron being so
serious and perceptive. He was usually such a
clown.

Aaron forced himself to smile. "Maybe you
and I should have come to the dance together.
We're spending most of it together anyway." He
stood up. "Let's pretend we're each other's date for

this last dance. That way we won't have to worry about what Todd and Jessica are doing." He held out his arms.

"OK." Elizabeth smiled. She put her arms around Aaron and they slow-danced to the romantic song coming from the gym.

"I really like this song," Aaron whispered. "Thanks for dancing with me."

Elizabeth looked up at Aaron. He was really sweet. And he was cute and charming, too. How could Jessica dump a great guy like Aaron to dance with Bruce Patman?

Suddenly Aaron's face was very close to hers. The next thing she knew, Aaron was kissing her, very softly—*right on the lips!*

There was a loud gasp behind them, and Aaron and Elizabeth broke apart in surprise and confusion.

"S-sorry," Caroline Pearce stammered, staring at them in amazement.

Aaron and Elizabeth stared back at her for a moment, not knowing what to do or say. Then Caroline ducked back into the gym.

Elizabeth shook her head, trying hard to collect her wits. She couldn't quite believe what had just happened. "This is terrible," she said tearfully. "Caroline is the biggest gossip in school. She'll tell everybody what she saw. Or what she *thought* she saw. I'd better talk to her and try to explain to her that it's not what it looks like."

"I'll come with you," Aaron offered. But just then the gym doors burst open and a mob of people came pouring out, forcing Aaron and Elizabeth apart and pushing them out the main door. There was no way to find Caroline now. There was no way to defend themselves.

The dance was over. And the damage was done.

Five

◇

Everywhere Elizabeth looked as she walked down the hall, she saw people whispering and darting furtive glances in her direction. It was only second period on Monday morning. *Caroline sure didn't waste any time spreading the story*, she thought angrily.

All day Sunday, Elizabeth had hoped that Caroline might keep her big mouth shut for once. She herself hadn't said anything to Jessica or Todd after the dance.

Aaron's father had driven all four of them home, and they had maintained a stony silence in the car and at the Wakefields' door.

Elizabeth had been furious with Todd for spending so much time with Veronica. And when

Todd saw how angry Elizabeth was, it made him angry that she was so angry at him. "I was just trying to be nice to Veronica," he had insisted over and over.

Aaron had been furious at Jessica as well, although Jessica had been too elated over Bruce's attentions to notice at first. But Aaron was so sullen on the drive home that soon Jessica was just as furious as everybody else.

At the front door, both couples had wished each other a curt and chilly good night.

This isn't how it was supposed to be at all, Elizabeth had found herself thinking sadly.

Once inside, Jessica had turned toward Elizabeth and shaken a finger at her warningly. "Don't say one word to me about Bruce and Aaron. Not one word." Then she had run up the stairs to her room.

Don't worry, Elizabeth had thought. *Who am I to criticize? I was the one kissing your date.* She hoped that Todd wouldn't find out. She hoped even more that Jessica wouldn't find out, though. Elizabeth didn't like keeping secrets from her twin, but this was something that she just didn't think Jessica would be able to understand or forgive.

When Elizabeth reached her locker, she saw that two of her friends, Sophia Rizzo and Sarah Thomas, were waiting for her. Seeing their surprised, curious expressions, Elizabeth knew that the story must be circulating quickly. It wouldn't be long before *everybody* knew.

"Is it true?" Sarah asked, wide-eyed.

"Is what true?" Elizabeth snapped irritatedly. She knew that neither Sarah nor Sophia had been at the dance. Their parents had taken both girls skiing for the weekend. All they knew about the dance was what they had heard. And apparently they had heard plenty.

Sarah and Sophia looked at each other. Then they looked back at Elizabeth.

"Is it true that you and Aaron were making out on the dance floor?" Sarah asked. "That's what I heard."

"And I heard that Jessica and Bruce Patman are a couple now," Sophia said.

"Was there really a fistfight?" Sarah asked.

"No! No! And no!" Elizabeth insisted. "Those are all dumb rumors started by Caroline Pearce. Nothing happened!"

"You mean there's nothing going on between you and Aaron?" Sophia asked.

"No!" Elizabeth cried.

"I don't care what you think!" they suddenly heard Jessica shout.

"I don't care what you think, either!" they heard Aaron answer.

Jessica and Aaron were coming down the hall, arguing at the top of their lungs. They were so angry that they weren't paying any attention to the fact that everyone in the hall was staring at them.

"If you think I'll ever go out with you again, you can forget it!" Aaron exploded.

"Fine!" Jessica yelled, stamping her foot. "From now on you can go out with Elizabeth, since you obviously like her so much better!"

Jessica stomped off and disappeared into a nearby classroom, while Aaron turned on his heel and stalked down the hall.

Sophia and Sarah both turned toward Elizabeth and raised their eyebrows skeptically.

"Nothing happened, huh?" Sophia said.

Todd tapped Elizabeth on the shoulder. "May I talk to you?" he asked in a very polite voice—*too* polite. Elizabeth had a bad feeling in the pit of her stomach as she turned to face him.

"Of course," she replied, trying to keep her voice neutral.

"Is it true?" he asked. "Did you really kiss Aaron at the dance?"

"Well, yes, but . . ."

Todd frowned and suddenly Elizabeth got angry at him all over again. "I wouldn't have been kissing Aaron if you hadn't been off dancing with Veronica all night," she snapped.

"I told you, I was just trying to be nice," he countered through gritted teeth.

"Well, you didn't have to be *that* nice," Elizabeth retorted.

"I thought you said that's what you liked about me," he shouted in frustration.

"I don't care what I said," Elizabeth shouted back. "You didn't have to dance the last four dances with Veronica. It certainly wasn't very nice of you to leave me standing all alone by the punch bowl!"

"You weren't alone," Todd reminded her. "You were with Aaron. Remember? As a matter of fact, it was *your* idea for us to go over and talk to him. I thought you were just being nice. But you probably wanted me out of the way so you could spend time with him."

Elizabeth was so angry she could hardly contain herself. "That is the stupidest thing I have ever heard in my whole life. How dare you accuse me of something like that? I don't know why I ever thought you were nice. You aren't nice at all!"

Todd glared at her through narrowed eyes for a moment. "Girls!" he said in disgust. Then he turned and marched away.

What a jerk! Elizabeth thought furiously. How could she ever have thought she liked him? She stomped into her next class, social studies. Unfortunately, it was Jessica's next class, too.

There was only one seat left unoccupied, and it was right next to Jessica. Elizabeth ignored Jessica's glare and threw herself into the seat. She slammed her books down on the desk.

All around her she could see shocked faces. Elizabeth hardly ever lost her temper, and her classmates didn't know how to react. Melissa McCormick stared at her with wide eyes. Maria Slater met her glance for a moment, and then hastily looked down at her lap. Elizabeth glanced around the classroom and saw several people nervously watching her and Jessica out of the corners of their eyes.

Mrs. Arnette, their teacher, had never been late for as long as Elizabeth could remember. But that day, the one day Elizabeth was hoping not to have to talk to anybody, Mrs. Arnette was nowhere to be seen.

Jessica leaned toward her. "So, did you kiss Aaron?" she hissed.

"I wouldn't have had a chance to kiss Aaron if you hadn't been off kissing Bruce," Elizabeth hissed back.

"Because of you, Aaron broke up with me," Jessica said angrily. "How could you kiss him when you knew I liked him?"

"If you like him so much, what were you doing with Bruce? It's your fault this whole mess started. It's because of you that Todd broke up with *me*."

"I just wish there were some way I could break up with *you*," Jessica raged under her breath.

"I feel exactly the same way," Elizabeth retorted in an undertone.

"Will you two please be quiet?" Amy said exasperatedly from behind them. "I think you should both get a grip. Ken's so embarrassed by the way everybody's acting that he told me this morning he doesn't want to have anything to do with girls and dating until the eighth grade. Thanks a bunch, *both* of you!"

That day at lunchtime, Elizabeth sat alone at a table, entertaining herself by throwing dirty looks at Jessica. Jessica sat with the Unicorns at the table they called the Unicorner, throwing dirty looks right back. Suddenly Jessica's face went red.

Elizabeth glanced up and saw Aaron standing right next to her with his tray. *OK, Jessica. Now watch this*, Elizabeth thought grimly. "Sit down," she said, trying to smile pleasantly at Aaron.

Aaron sat down next to her. "I heard about what Jessica said to you," he began. "And I also heard about Todd. I'm really sorry about everything. Would it help if I tried to explain things to Jessica and Todd, or apologized to them, maybe? Jessica might not have acted like a very good date, but I guess I didn't, either. It was my idea to dance with you," he mumbled, his face flushing, "and . . . and everything. It's not fair for anybody to be mad at you."

Elizabeth was touched. Aaron looked genuinely worried about her. She could see he felt bad about what had happened and wanted to help her —unlike Todd, who just wanted to yell at her and make things worse.

"Thanks," she said gratefully. "But it's not your fault. You don't need to apologize to anybody. Besides," she said, catching sight of Jessica's angry face, "I *liked* dancing with you."

Aaron caught Elizabeth's quick look in Jessica's direction and his face darkened. "I liked dancing with you, too," he said belligerently, as if he were really talking to Jessica.

Just then both Aaron and Elizabeth saw Bruce wave at Jessica. Jessica quickly hopped up and went over to Bruce's table. The next thing Elizabeth and Aaron knew, she was laughing loudly and tossing her head, flipping her hair back off her shoulder every two seconds.

Aaron's mouth tightened for a moment. Then he turned to Elizabeth with a big smile. "So what did you think of the picture Mr. Sweeney drew in art class last week? Wasn't that nerdy-looking?" He burst into laughter.

Elizabeth was puzzled for a moment. Aaron sure seemed to have a changeable personality. Why was he suddenly making fun of Mr. Sweeney? Then Elizabeth saw him shoot another look in Jessica's direction and she understood. Aaron was trying to show Jessica that he was doing just fine without her.

A moment later Todd walked by. He never even turned to look at Elizabeth. He just walked straight over to the table where Veronica was sitting and sat down beside her.

Elizabeth's own face fell for a moment. Then she heard Aaron laugh again. *Well, if Aaron can show Jessica he doesn't care, I can show Todd that I don't care, either,* Elizabeth thought grimly. She turned to Aaron. "Mr. Sweeney can be such a nerd sometimes," she agreed. "Remember the time he spilled that bright green paint all over Jerry McAllister?"

At that, Elizabeth and Aaron both burst into loud laughter.

At that moment Amy Sutton passed by with her tray and noticed Elizabeth and Aaron laughing hysterically. "What's so funny?" she asked them.

"Nothing!" Elizabeth snapped.

Six

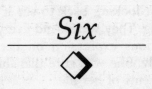

"You are sooooo lucky," Ellen Riteman breathed enviously. "Bruce is mega-adorable."

"I'm so totally jealous." Kimberly sighed. "Bruce is definitely the best-looking guy in school."

"We're very proud of you, Jessica," Janet said with a smile. "This looks great for the Unicorns."

Jessica wiggled her toes happily. She was loving every minute of her friends' praise. Bruce Patman's attention had definitely given Jessica's prestige a boost in the Unicorns' eyes.

Classes were over for the day and the Unicorns were standing in front of the school, waiting for Bruce to meet Jessica. During lunch that day he had asked her if she wanted to go to Casey's with him after school to get ice cream. The Unicorns had discussed it thoroughly all afternoon and agreed that it counted as a date.

"Hey, Jessica," Bruce called out as he came through the door. "Ready to hit Casey's?"

"Sure," Jessica replied brightly. She waved at her friends and fell into step with Bruce. Jessica couldn't resist looking back to see if the Unicorns were watching. They were. And every one of them wore an envious expression on her face. Jessica sighed happily. She was sure that this was one of the best moments of her life.

"You should have heard me today in my history class," Bruce said. "I really got off a couple of good ones. You know, I bet I'm the funniest guy in the seventh grade."

"I'll bet you are, too," Jessica agreed. "You know who else is funny? I think—"

"I even made the teacher laugh," Bruce interrupted. "You *know* you're on a roll when you can make the teacher laugh."

Jessica smiled. "I made the teacher laugh once," she said. "It was Mr. Sweeney. I told him I—"

Bruce stopped abruptly in front of a plate-glass window and checked his hair in the reflection. "Uh-huh," he said absently as he smoothed down the top.

Jessica waited for him to ask what she had done to make Mr. Sweeney laugh. But he seemed to have forgotten she had been talking.

"You know, a couple of people have told me I look like Johnny Buck, the rock star. What do you think?"

Jessica frowned, studying his face. "A little bit, I guess."

"A little bit!" Bruce exclaimed, looking crest-fallen. Jessica knew immediately that she had made a blunder.

"I was just kidding," she corrected herself quickly, giving him her most dazzling smile. "You look *exactly* like Johnny Buck. I've always thought so."

Bruce looked pleased. "Really?"

"Oh, absolutely," Jessica said firmly.

Bruce took her hand as the two of them walked into Casey's and sat down in a booth. The place was packed with Sweet Valley Middle School students. Jessica was glad there were so many people there to see her and Bruce together.

The waiter came over and Bruce ordered. "A banana split—to split." He laughed loudly at his own humor.

What a dumb joke, Jessica thought. Then she felt bad. *How many girls get the opportunity to be seen with Bruce Patman?* she asked herself. It was a real honor. She shouldn't ruin it by being negative. Jessica forced herself to giggle.

The bell on the door tinkled, and Aaron and Elizabeth came in together. As soon as they saw Jessica and Bruce they looked startled and hesitated

at the door. Jessica saw Elizabeth whisper something to Aaron. They looked uncertainly in Jessica's
direction again, as if debating whether or not to
stay.

Jessica felt herself getting angrier and angrier
as she watched them together. *I'll show them how
much I care.* As soon as Jessica thought Elizabeth
and Aaron were looking, she smiled as brightly as
she could and leaned closer to Bruce. "You are so
funny, Bruce," she told him loudly, fluttering her
eyelashes flirtatiously.

Aaron and Elizabeth whispered together again.
Then they headed for another booth and sat down,
carefully avoiding looking at Jessica.

All around Casey's, Jessica could feel people
watching her. Melissa and Sophia sat at the
counter, glancing over their shoulders. Mandy and
Mary were in a corner booth, watching the scene
eagerly.

Jessica knew she couldn't afford to look angry
or upset. If she did, people might think Aaron had
dumped her for Elizabeth. She wanted to be sure
that everyone—including Aaron and Elizabeth—
knew that Aaron was the one who had been
dumped.

But as Jessica leaned forward again to flirt with
Bruce, she saw Aaron and Elizabeth reach across
the table—*and hold hands!*

A buzz of excited conversation circulated
quickly around Casey's. Suddenly Jessica heard

Caroline Pearce gasp. "There's Todd!" Caroline exclaimed in a loud stage whisper.

Jessica almost gasped herself when she saw Todd walk in with Veronica. Todd barely glanced over at Elizabeth, but Veronica gave her a long, smug, victorious look. Jessica couldn't help feeling a flash of pity for her twin. *Elizabeth really looks pathetic now*, she thought.

But Elizabeth didn't seem to mind at all. She was too busy laughing at something Aaron had just said.

Jessica shrugged angrily. *What do I care? I've got Bruce Patman.* She fixed her gaze on Bruce and stared adoringly into his eyes. She laughed and tossed her hair off her shoulder.

Bruce frowned. "What are you laughing at?" he asked. "I didn't say anything."

"Oh," Jessica said. "Sorry."

Later that night, the twins and their parents were sitting in the living room after dinner. Jessica sat on the sofa flipping through a fashion magazine, and Mr. and Mrs. Wakefield were both reading the newspaper.

Elizabeth sat on the floor, pretending to study her history textbook. Normally she preferred to do her homework in her room. But that evening she felt too down and lonely to be by herself.

She couldn't get her mind off that afternoon at Casey's. Todd had acted as if he was having the time of his life with Veronica. She wondered if it was possible that he'd just been acting the whole time. After all, she had been acting as if she was having a great time with Aaron when she wasn't. Not that she didn't like Aaron. He was really nice, even if he did talk about soccer all the time.

"Isn't one of you going to answer the phone?" she heard her father ask impatiently.

Elizabeth looked up, startled. She suddenly became aware of the ringing telephone. Jessica was looking startled, too. *Her mind must be on Bruce,* Elizabeth thought.

The telephone rang again, but Elizabeth didn't make a move to answer it. She really didn't feel like talking to anybody. And from the looks of it, neither did Jessica.

The phone rang again. "Oh, good grief," Mr. Wakefield muttered grumpily. "Usually they're knocking each other down to get to the phone." He got up and went to answer the phone in the kitchen.

They heard his voice murmuring in the kitchen for a moment. "It's Aaron," he said, returning and sinking back down into his chair.

Jessica and Elizabeth looked at each other. Then they looked expectantly at their father.

"What?" he said. "What? What's that look?"

"Who does he want to talk to?" Jessica asked.

Mrs. Wakefield glanced up from her reading. "I

think your father is assuming that he wants to speak to you," she said, looking curiously at Jessica.

"Would you please ask him?" Jessica said.

Mr. Wakefield sighed heavily and stood up again. In a few seconds he came back with a surprised look on his face. "He wants to speak to Elizabeth."

Elizabeth watched Jessica's face carefully for signs of disappointment. But if Jessica was disappointed, she didn't let it show. Elizabeth got up from the floor and went to the telephone.

"Hello," she said.

"Hi," she heard Aaron's voice say over the line. "It's me, Aaron."

"I know," Elizabeth said. "How are you?"

"Fine," Aaron responded. "How are you?"

"Fine," Elizabeth answered.

There was a long pause. Elizabeth tapped her foot impatiently. "So," she said at last. "What did you do this afternoon after we left Casey's?"

"Not much," Aaron replied.

Elizabeth sighed. However talkative Aaron was in person, he didn't seem to have much to say on the telephone.

"Well, I guess I'll see you tomorrow," Aaron said finally. "So long."

"Good-bye," Elizabeth said, hanging up the phone.

I wonder why he called. Elizabeth chewed on her lip. Then she realized it must be part of this boy-girl stuff. They were a couple now, and that meant Aaron felt he had to call—whether he had anything to say or not. Elizabeth went back into the living room. She hoped Aaron wouldn't feel he had to call *every* night.

She threw herself down on the floor and moodily flipped the pages of her book. Then she let out a soft sigh. Todd wasn't as funny or as outgoing as Aaron, but at least you could have a real conversation with him. She hated to admit it, but she missed him.

The phone rang again, and they could hear Steven answer it in the hall upstairs. A few moments later, he came thumping down the steps and stuck his head into the living room. "Oh, Jessica," he teased. "Guess who's on the phone? The mighty Bruce Patman. Way to go, shrimp!"

"Knock it off, Steven," Jessica said shortly as she went to take the phone call in the kitchen. "You're such a jerk sometimes," she added as she brushed past him.

Steven stared after her with his mouth open. "What'd I say? What'd I do? I thought Bruce Patman was supposed to be hot stuff." He looked at Elizabeth as if waiting for an explanation.

"Why are you asking me?" Elizabeth shouted. "I don't know why Jessica does the things she does. I'm not her keeper. So mind your own business!"

"Elizabeth!" Mrs. Wakefield said sharply.

"That's no way to speak to your brother. What has gotten into you and your sister these days?"

Suddenly a lump formed in Elizabeth's throat. "I'm sorry," she muttered. Then, as her family watched in amazement, Elizabeth ran out of the room, up the stairs, and into her room. She slammed the door with a loud bang.

I hate Jessica, she thought angrily. *I hate Bruce. I hate Veronica. And I hate Todd, too!* Elizabeth tore the locket from around her neck and threw it angrily onto her night table.

Then she flopped down on her bed and burst into tears.

Seven

"Jake Hamilton has called me every single night since the dance," Lila said smugly. "Some nights he calls me twice."

"Peter put a rose on my desk." Mandy blushed. "Isn't that romantic?"

Jessica sat at the Unicorner on Friday afternoon listening to her friends giggle and brag about their boyfriends. Ever since the dance, it seemed that all they talked about was boys, boys, boys. It was actually getting kind of boring—almost as boring as listening to Bruce, Jessica thought unhappily.

Bruce called her every night, too. The previous night, they had talked for almost an hour. Or more accurately, *Bruce* had talked for almost an hour—

mostly about Bruce. Jessica couldn't think of a single question he had asked her about herself.

It was really weird. A week earlier, Jessica would have died for a chance to listen to Bruce talk about himself. Now she was sick of it. *Am I crazy?* she wondered.

"Has Bruce called you, Jessica?" Janet asked.

All the girls fell silent and stared at Jessica with bated breath.

"He calls me every night," Jessica replied.

They all let out their breath in an envious sigh.

Jessica felt as if she was riding on an emotional seesaw. Her spirits soared when she realized how much the other Unicorns admired and envied her. But they plummeted when she realized that the only way she could keep up her image was by having Bruce as her boyfriend.

"Unbelievable," Kimberly said, shaking her head. "I'd give anything to have Bruce Patman calling me."

Jessica looked around at her friends. Nothing she had ever done or said had impressed them as much as this had. No matter how tired she got of listening to Bruce, she could never break up with him. Besides, everybody had a boyfriend these days. It would be awful to be the only Unicorn who didn't.

When she looked over and saw Aaron and Elizabeth walk into the cafeteria together, she couldn't help wishing that Aaron was her boyfriend instead of Bruce. Aaron was funny and friendly. And he listened, too. He always laughed at Jessica's jokes. Whenever Jessica tried to make a joke around Bruce, he either pretended he didn't get it or interrupted before she got to the punch line.

Jessica looked up again and saw Aaron and Elizabeth laughing and talking together. Suddenly, Jessica felt just awful. "Excuse me," she choked out, rising from the table.

"Anything wrong?" Mandy asked.

"No," Jessica said quickly. "I just need to get something from my locker." There was no way she could sit there any longer and watch Aaron and Elizabeth together. It made her too unhappy.

"I know how you feel," a voice said behind her as she left the cafeteria.

Jessica turned and saw Veronica Brooks smiling knowingly at her.

"What are you talking about?" Jessica demanded.

"If my sister stole my boyfriend, I'd be really upset, too," Veronica said.

"Elizabeth didn't steal my boyfriend," Jessica muttered. "Bruce is my boyfriend."

Veronica touched Jessica's arm sympathetically. "Sure," she said. "Whatever you say. I just somehow had the idea that you really liked Aaron. I mean, wasn't he supposed to be *your* date for the dance?"

"Yes," Jessica admitted grudgingly. "He was."

"It looks to me as if Elizabeth was just biding her time, waiting for you to dance a couple of times with somebody else before she moved in."

Jessica sighed impatiently. "That's not true," she answered grumpily. She didn't really believe that Elizabeth was that calculating. She and Aaron had been thrown together at the dance, and it had given them the chance to find out they liked each other. *It's my own fault,* she thought miserably. *If I hadn't gone running after Bruce, they never would have gotten together.*

"She's a smart girl," Veronica reminded Jessica. "And she's used to getting what she wants. Aren't you being just a little naive?"

Maybe it was because she was so miserable. Or maybe it was because she hated admitting that her problems might be her own fault. But all of a sudden Jessica began to see her sister in a new and sinister light.

Maybe, just maybe, Veronica was right. Maybe Elizabeth really had been after Aaron from the beginning. The more Jessica thought about it, the more it all made sense.

Elizabeth really stabbed me in the back, Jessica thought bitterly. *She's always known I liked Aaron. And she stole him anyway—the first chance she got!*

"Poor Todd." Veronica shook her head. "If it hadn't been for me, he would have been left out in the cold."

"That's right," Jessica said. "He would have. And he's a nice guy, too. Elizabeth really treated him badly."

Veronica sighed. "It must be hard to have a sister who's always getting credit for being so great, when you know what she's really like."

"It is. Nobody ever sees the bad side of Elizabeth."

"Except you," Veronica said.

"That's right," Jessica agreed. "Except me."

Veronica leaned back against the lockers, apparently thinking hard. "And even when you tell people about Elizabeth, they probably don't believe you. Why would they? She's always getting good grades and acting like such a goody-goody. But who knows what she's really thinking and doing?"

Jessica had the feeling that the conversation was suddenly veering away from reality. But she didn't care. It felt so good to say bad things about Elizabeth just then. It was a relief to believe that Elizabeth was in the wrong for a change instead of her.

Veronica put her arm around Jessica's shoulders. "I think you and I are the only two people at Sweet Valley Middle School who see Elizabeth for what she really is."

Jessica didn't really like having Veronica's arm around her shoulders. But it was nice having somebody take her side against Elizabeth.

"You're right," Jessica said with a nod. "We are the only two people who see her for what she is."

"Maybe if we put our heads together," Veronica whispered conspiratorially, "we can change that."

Doesn't he ever talk about anything but soccer? Elizabeth wondered as she and Aaron were walking to their classes after lunch.

"You know what else I like about soccer?" Aaron was saying. "It's a game of skill, not just strength. You have to really think about what you're doing and why."

"Mm-hmm," Elizabeth responded automatically. She wasn't really listening. She was watching Veronica and Jessica whisper together by the water fountain.

That's strange, she thought. *What do Jessica and Veronica have in common all of a sudden?*

When they looked up and saw her, Elizabeth knew. Two pairs of eyes glared angrily in her direction. They were so unfriendly that Elizabeth felt herself growing pale. What they had in common was that neither of them liked her.

"So I'll see you later," Aaron said.

Elizabeth tried to smile in spite of the sinking feeling in her stomach. "OK," she said quietly. "I'll see you."

Just then Amy came out of the girls' bathroom, and Elizabeth grabbed her arm.

"Hey," Amy cried in surprise.

"Sorry," Elizabeth said, steering her down the hall. "But I need to talk to you."

"Well, I don't know," Amy said. "Are you finished playing stupid dating games with Aaron and Todd and Bruce and Jessica and Veronica and—" Amy frowned. "Did I leave anybody out?"

Elizabeth couldn't help smiling. "No, I think that's it. Believe me, I'd love to stop playing games. I just haven't figured out how. Please don't be mad at me anymore."

Amy shrugged and smiled. "I'm not. Not really. So, what's up?"

Elizabeth sighed. "I'm not sure. But Jessica and Veronica are looking awfully chummy all of a sudden."

"So let them be chummy," Amy said. "What do you care?"

"Veronica seems like such a troublemaker. It's obvious she doesn't like me. And you know how Jessica can be when she's mad."

"Don't worry about them," Amy reassured her. "There's nothing they can do to you. If you really want something to worry about, worry about me." Amy laughed. "Ken hasn't said one word to me since Monday morning. And I just heard that Ellen is having a boy-girl party for Valentine's Day. It's next Friday night—and it's a dance!"

"*Another* one?" Elizabeth groaned.

"*Another* one."

Eight

◇

"Shh." Jessica put her finger to her lips. "I think I hear her leaving."

Jessica and Veronica had been sitting in Jessica's room whispering about Elizabeth ever since they got home from school.

Out in the upstairs hall, they heard Elizabeth close her door and walk down the stairs. Veronica and Jessica ran to the door of Jessica's room and opened it a crack.

"Bye, Mom. I'm going over to Amy's," they heard Elizabeth shout from the front door. "My homework's all finished."

"All right, honey," Mrs. Wakefield's voice answered faintly. "Be home in time for dinner."

"Here's our chance," Veronica said eagerly. "I've got a great idea. Let's go in her room."

Jessica hesitated. "I don't know . . ." she began uneasily. It was one thing to bring Veronica home and say nasty things about Elizabeth behind her back. It was another thing to let Veronica into Elizabeth's room without her permission.

"Looks like Elizabeth's not the only goody-goody in the family." Veronica laughed nastily.

"I am not a goody-goody," Jessica protested. "I'm a Unicorn. We're wild," she said proudly.

"Then prove it," Veronica challenged.

"I don't have to," Jessica insisted.

Veronica shook her head. "You Unicorns are all talk. At my old school, I was one of the in crowd. We were *really* wild. We didn't just have geeky school dances—we had real kissing parties. We weren't like you goody-goodies at Sweet Valley."

Veronica leaned back and smiled wistfully. "And we knew how to be mean," she continued. "At my old school, the girls from the in crowd didn't get mad, they got even."

Jessica twirled a few strands of hair indecisively.

"Are you going to let yourself be intimidated by Miss Perfect all your life?" Veronica asked condescendingly.

"Of course not," Jessica snapped.

"Then get even with her," Veronica said. "It'll

teach her a lesson. Elizabeth needs to be taken down a peg or two. She's been asking for it."

Veronica had a point, Jessica decided. Besides, she didn't want Veronica to think she was a wimp. "OK," she said. "Let's go."

Soon she and Veronica were creeping around Elizabeth's room. "I need to find her math homework first," Veronica said, rifling through the papers and notebooks on Elizabeth's desk. "Ah-hah," she exclaimed with satisfaction. "Here it is."

Jessica watched Veronica's face as she looked over the math problems. Her eyes turned cold and narrow, and Jessica felt a little pang of foreboding. Veronica studied the paper for several minutes and then nodded. "All these answers are right," she said.

"Wow! You must be as good in math as Elizabeth." Jessica was impressed. It would have taken her hours to figure out all those problems.

Veronica smiled and reached for a pencil. "When this assignment gets handed back, I'll be *better* in math than Elizabeth." She began to erase some of Elizabeth's homework.

"What are you doing?" Jessica asked.

"Just changing a couple of the answers," Veronica said. She very carefully and slowly penciled in new answers. She imitated Elizabeth's writing so well that it would be impossible for anyone, even Elizabeth, to tell that anything had been altered. "Miss Perfect is going to get a big surprise when she finds out that some of her answers are wrong." She laughed nastily and put the homework back in Elizabeth's notebook.

"Now," she said briskly, "let's see what else we can do. Does Elizabeth keep a diary? It would be fun to see if she has any dirty little secrets." Veronica opened the drawer of Elizabeth's desk and began pawing through it.

Jessica suddenly felt sick watching Veronica's eager face as she snooped in Elizabeth's desk. This was wrong and she knew it. No matter what Elizabeth had done, going through her desk behind her back was a terrible thing to do.

"Stop," she cried out.

Veronica looked up at her in surprise. "Why?"

"We've done enough, changing the answers to her homework and all," Jessica answered edgily. "I don't think we should look through her private stuff."

Veronica waved Jessica's protests aside. Then she turned back to the drawer and pulled out Elizabeth's journal.

"Don't," Jessica said, holding out her hand for the journal. "Give it to me."

But Veronica began turning the pages. "Don't be such a chicken. This was your idea as much as mine."

Jessica began to feel like the biggest traitor in the world. She rushed over and snatched the journal from Veronica.

"Hey," Veronica objected. Her hand shot out and closed over the book, and the two girls began to play tug of war. "Let go," Veronica demanded.

"You let go," Jessica said through gritted teeth.

Veronica's hand slipped and Jessica stumbled backwards. She dropped the journal, and several loose pages came spilling out onto the floor.

"Now look what you've done," Veronica said angrily. "I don't understand you, Jessica. I really don't. First you tell me you want to get back at Elizabeth, and then when I show you how to do it, you turn chicken."

Jessica quickly began to gather up the papers. "Sorry," she muttered.

Veronica sighed impatiently and began to wander restlessly around Elizabeth's room while Jessica put the papers back in order. *I wish she'd go home*, Jessica thought. Her new friend was beginning to give her the creeps. Now Veronica was snooping around Elizabeth's night table, picking things up and examining them curiously.

One of the loose papers on the floor caught Jessica's eye. It was an essay Elizabeth had written the previous year. The title was "Why My Sister Is My Best Friend."

Jessica felt like crying. Elizabeth really was her best friend. How could she be doing this to her?

As Jessica carefully replaced the paper in the journal she came to a decision. It was time to tell

Veronica to leave. She stood up, and as she did she saw Veronica slip something into her pocket.

Jessica gasped. Veronica whirled around and saw Jessica staring at her open-mouthed.

"If I were you," Veronica said, "I wouldn't say a word to anybody about this." Her tone was vaguely threatening, and Jessica swallowed nervously.

Veronica took a step in her direction, and Jessica involuntarily backed away. "Don't forget, Jessica, there's no way you can tell on me without telling on yourself. That wouldn't make either one of us look very good, would it?"

She's right, Jessica thought miserably. *I can't warn Elizabeth about her homework or anything without looking like a real rat.* Veronica had her, and they both knew it.

"I'd better get home," Veronica said. "I'll see you next week at school." She walked to the door and paused, turning to face Jessica. "Remember, this is our secret." Then she left.

Jessica let out her breath with a sigh of relief. Veronica was the most horrible girl she had ever met. How could she have thought she wanted to be friends with her?

Jessica hurried over to Elizabeth's night table to see if she could figure out what Veronica had taken. It was impossible to tell. Jessica didn't know what had been on her sister's night table to begin with.

It was probably just a lipstick or something, Jessica thought, trying to shrug it off. *I guess it doesn't really matter*. Her conscience pricked at her over the math homework. *Oh well*, she thought, shrugging that off, too. *How much damage can a couple of wrong answers do? Elizabeth is in pretty solid with Ms. Wyler.*

The phone rang and Jessica hurried to answer it.

"Hello?" she said.

"It's me," Lila said breathlessly. "Have you heard the news?"

"What news?" Jessica asked.

"Ellen told us at lunch, but you had already left. She's having a party next Friday for Valentine's Day."

"A boy-girl party?" Jessica asked with a sinking heart.

"Yes. Isn't that great?"

"Definitely," Jessica responded, trying to sound enthusiastic. "It's just great."

Nine

◇

"The highest grade in the class went to Veronica, with ninety-nine percent," Ms. Wyler announced on Tuesday. "Congratulations, Veronica."

Veronica accepted her math homework with a big smile.

"There was a lot of good work on this assignment," Ms. Wyler continued. "Amy, nice job."

"Thanks, Ms. Wyler," Amy said proudly.

"Mandy, here's yours. Well done."

Ms. Wyler continued to return the assignments, and for most people she had a smile and a compliment.

Elizabeth eagerly waited her turn. The homework had been easy and she felt pretty sure she'd gotten all the answers right.

Finally, Ms. Wyler had only one paper left in her hand. Elizabeth began to smile in anticipation. But her smile faded when she saw the serious look on Ms. Wyler's face.

"See me after class," she said softly but sternly. She put the paper on Elizabeth's desk and then walked briskly to the front of the room.

There was a stunned silence. Every eye was on Elizabeth. She felt her face flushing deep red—almost as red as the glaring red marks on her paper and the big red circled F. She was sure her grade was visible to every single person in the room. She wished Ms. Wyler had put the paper on her desk face down.

"Who's interested in fractions?" Ms. Wyler asked, breaking the long, uncomfortable silence.

"Nobody," Aaron joked, a little too loudly.

The whole class erupted into nervous laughter, except for Elizabeth. She was still staring down at her returned homework in horror.

She noticed Amy giving her a surprised look. "What happened?" Amy mouthed.

Elizabeth shook her head. She was too shocked and humiliated to answer. The problems had seemed so simple when she did them. How was it possible that she had gotten so many wrong?

Math class seemed to go on forever. When it was finally over and the other kids had filed out, Elizabeth approached Ms. Wyler's desk.

"Elizabeth," Ms. Wyler said. "What happened here?"

Elizabeth shook her head. "I don't know," she whispered. "I can't understand how I made so many mistakes. I know how to solve these problems. In fact, it took me hardly any time to do them. They were easy."

Ms. Wyler tapped her fingers thoughtfully on the desk. "Sometimes when an assignment is too easy for a student, that student tends to rush through it and get sloppy. I don't like that, Elizabeth. When I give these assignments, I expect you to take your time and do them right. Please don't let this happen again. Math is not about being fast. It's about being accurate."

"I'm sorry," Elizabeth said softly. She hurried out of the classroom feeling as if she might burst into tears.

"It was really weird," Mandy exclaimed. "Elizabeth usually does great in math, but she totally blew her homework this week."

"She did?" Jessica tried to sound surprised. She and Mandy were sitting alone at the Unicorner waiting for the other girls to arrive.

"Yeah," Mandy said. "Elizabeth usually gets the highest grade in the class. I was sitting right behind her and I saw her paper. She got an F."

"An F!" Jessica shrieked. She felt terrible. She had had no idea that Veronica had changed so many answers. "That's awful. I thought she'd just get a B or something." She shut her mouth with a snap when she realized what she'd just said.

"What do you mean?" Mandy asked. "How did you know she wouldn't get an A? Is something the matter?"

"No," Jessica answered quickly. "She's just, um . . ." She glanced in her sister's direction. Elizabeth was sitting with Aaron at a table in the corner of the room. The two of them were deep in conversation.

Mandy caught the look and smiled. "I get it. She's having a hard time concentrating. Romance can do that to you."

Jessica knew her face was falling into a frown, but she couldn't help it.

Mandy noticed Jessica's unhappy expression. "You don't mind, do you?" Mandy asked. "I mean about Elizabeth and Aaron. After all, you've got Bruce, right?"

"Sure," Jessica said softly. "He's really great." But she couldn't help looking over in Aaron's direction one more time.

"You don't sound very happy," Mandy said. "Aren't you thrilled about having a chance to be with Bruce at Ellen's party?"

Gag! Jessica thought. She grimaced at the prospect of spending a whole evening with Bruce. He had become so unbearable that she was actually avoiding him these days, ducking into classrooms and around corners when she saw him coming.

She knew now that she would much rather be with Aaron than with Bruce. She darted another glance in Elizabeth's direction. This time she caught Elizabeth sneaking a look at Todd. She saw a tiny expression of unhappiness flicker over her sister's face. It was there for only an instant before Elizabeth turned her attention back to Aaron. Still, Jessica was sure she had seen it.

I wonder if Elizabeth would really rather be with Todd than with Aaron, she thought. *Maybe she just got stuck with Aaron like I got stuck with Bruce.*

But even if Elizabeth wasn't crazy about Aaron, Aaron seemed to be crazy about Elizabeth. Jessica watched him closely as he talked and laughed and clowned around. Then he suddenly turned and caught Jessica staring. Their eyes met, and for a brief moment Aaron's face took on a hopeful expression. Then his face went blank and he turned quickly back toward Elizabeth.

Hmm, thought Jessica. *Maybe Aaron isn't so crazy about Elizabeth after all. Maybe he still likes me.*

Jessica's mind began to work furiously. After what she had done to Elizabeth, she owed her something. And she had a feeling that the best thing she could do for Elizabeth would be to get her back together with Todd. That would be getting even with Veronica, too, she realized happily. And if she could manage to get Aaron back for herself, everything would be perfect again.

The problem was how to do it. She could try to talk to Todd and tell him that Elizabeth didn't really like Aaron, but Todd probably wouldn't believe her. He would think she was just trying to get Aaron back. The only person he would believe was Elizabeth. And Elizabeth was much too proud to talk to him herself.

"Jessica? Jessica?"

Jessica was suddenly aware that Mandy was speaking to her. She had been so lost in thought, she hadn't been paying attention. "I'm sorry," she said quickly. "What did you say?"

"I was just asking what you're going to wear to Ellen's party," Mandy said.

Jessica smiled. The perfect solution had just come to her.

"Knock knock," Aaron said.

A frown wrinkled Elizabeth's forehead as she chewed her sandwich thoughtfully.

"Knock knock," Aaron said again.

Was it just her imagination, Elizabeth wondered, or did Jessica keep looking over at Aaron? This was the third time she'd caught her twin glancing in their direction.

"Elizabeth," Aaron said. "Are you listening?" He reached over and gently shook Elizabeth's arm, startling her out of her thoughts.

"Oh." She smiled. "I'm sorry. My mind was just on something else."

"I was trying to tell you a joke," Aaron complained, sounding hurt.

Elizabeth did her best to look interested. "What's the joke?"

Aaron sighed. "Never mind. You don't really seem to be in the mood for jokes. Are you still upset about blowing your math homework?"

"No," Elizabeth answered. "I was, but I'm not anymore. It taught me not to do my homework in such a big hurry." She pushed back her chair. "I'll be right back, Aaron. I need to get some more milk." Elizabeth got up and headed toward the lunch line.

"Too bad about that math grade," a voice said behind her. Elizabeth turned and saw Veronica giving her a spiteful smile. "Looks like you're not number one anymore. Not with Ms. Wyler. Not with Todd." She raised her eyebrows. "And not with Aaron, either," she added pointedly.

"What are you talking about?" Elizabeth demanded.

Veronica laughed nastily. "Look at him."

Elizabeth looked over and saw that Aaron was sneaking looks in Jessica's direction. "Seems like every time I see Aaron, he's looking at Jessica," Veronica said. "Maybe he doesn't like you as much as you think he does."

Veronica didn't know it, but this was the best

news Elizabeth had had all day. If Aaron still liked Jessica, and Jessica still liked Aaron, then it was time to get them back together. Elizabeth had heard enough soccer stories and knock-knock jokes to last her the rest of her life.

"Remember that when you and Aaron are dancing at Ellen's party," Veronica hissed. Then she quickly walked away.

Elizabeth shook her head in disbelief. She had never met anybody as determined to be her enemy as Veronica was. In fact, it seemed as if everybody was determined to be enemies these days. Elizabeth and Jessica. Elizabeth and Todd. Jessica and Aaron. If only they all could talk and get things straightened out. She was sick of being angry at everybody.

She watched as Veronica sat down with Todd at the lunch table and began to chatter away. Todd didn't look Elizabeth's way at all. *He really doesn't like me anymore,* she thought sadly.

There was no way she could talk to Todd, she decided. Someday maybe he would see the real Veronica. In the meantime, Elizabeth had to concentrate on getting her sister back together with Aaron.

"What are you looking so thoughtful about?" Amy asked, walking up.

Elizabeth sighed. "I'm still trying to figure out some way to win the dating game."

"Come up with anything good?" Amy asked with a grin.

"No." Elizabeth smiled. "But I'm working on it."

"Me too," Amy said. "I've got an appointment with Kimberly and Lila this afternoon for another makeover. Want to come watch?"

"You're going to try *another* new look?"

"They say clothes make the woman," Amy reminded her with a shrug.

"That's right." Elizabeth nodded. Then she thought about what Amy had just said. It was too early to tell, but Elizabeth thought Amy might just have given her a brilliant idea.

Ten

"What do you think?" Kimberly asked, stepping back to admire her work.

"It looks great," Lila exclaimed. "Really sixties. What do you think, Elizabeth?"

"It's very, um . . ." Elizabeth was at a loss for words.

Amy went to the mirror and turned one way and then another. "I don't know. It's not exactly *me*," she said doubtfully.

The four girls were gathered in Lila's opulent bedroom for Amy's latest makeover. Kimberly and Lila had been working feverishly for over an hour. They had made Amy try on dozens of outfits, and the discarded skirts, pants, blouses, and belts lay scattered around the room.

"You really think Ken's going to like this look?" Amy asked. She stepped back to take in her entire reflection. She was wearing a headband around her forehead, faded bell-bottom blue jeans that had belonged to Kimberly's mother, and a fringed vest that Lila had bought in a vintage cloth-ing store.

"I told you, I saw Ken in the record store last week," Lila said. "He was buying this *Best of the Sixties* CD. I heard him and Peter DeHaven talking about the girl on the cover, and Ken said she looked really cool. She was dressed just like you are now." Lila gave a satisfied nod. "You know, I think maybe I'll be a costume designer when I grow up. This was really fun."

Amy looked at herself doubtfully. "Fun for you. But I'm afraid I'll feel stupid walking around in public like this."

"Hold still for a minute," Kimberly said. She grabbed an eyeliner pencil and carefully drew a peace sign on Amy's cheek. "You don't have any choice, Amy. Ellen's party is tomorrow night. If you're going to get Ken to change his mind about dating, you're going to have to do it fast."

"I just can't imagine wearing this to school to-morrow," Amy said.

"Why not?" Kimberly demanded. "Come on, dare to be different. You could start a trend."

Amy plucked at the fringe on her vest. "I don't know. I just don't think I'm the trendsetting type.

Maybe I should give it a trial run first. I could wear it someplace this afternoon and see how it goes."

"Wear it to the drugstore," Elizabeth suggested. The drugstore was huge, with a soda fountain, a card counter, lots of gifts, and a great selection of candy. "We have to go buy Valentine's Day cards, remember?"

"Good idea," Amy said. "Then if I feel totally ridiculous in this outfit, I won't be stuck in it all day at school."

"Amy," Lila said with an impatient sigh, "you've got to learn to be bold when it comes to fashion."

"If you're so bold, how come you guys aren't wearing outfits like this?" Amy asked.

"Because we already have dates to Ellen's party," Kimberly said with a giggle.

"Now come downstairs, Amy," Lila said. "I want to iron your hair."

"What?" Amy exclaimed.

"Kimberly's mom said that when she was a teenager in the sixties, she ironed her hair to make it straight. I already asked Mrs. Pervis to set up the ironing board downstairs." Mrs. Pervis was the Fowlers' housekeeper.

"Hold it," Amy said. "I hate to break it to you guys, but my hair is already straight."

"Yeah." Lila eyed Amy with a professional air. "But it's kind of sticking out on the sides. What we're going for is the curtain look. You know, hair that falls straight down like a curtain."

Amy began to back away. "Don't think I'm not grateful for all your help. But you guys are nuts if you think I'm going to let you near my head with a hot iron."

"Don't worry," Lila assured her. "Mrs. Pervis said she knows how to do it. She'll make sure I don't singe off your hair."

"Singe off my hair!" Amy shrieked in alarm. "Forget it!"

"But Amy," Kimberly began.

"I said forget it," Amy said decisively.

"OK, then." Lila sighed. "But don't come crying to us when you don't have a date for the party."

The drugstore was packed when Amy and Elizabeth got there. Everywhere they looked, they saw kids they knew buying cards and boxes of candy.

Maybe I should send Todd a valentine, Elizabeth thought. It might be a good way of letting him know she still liked him without having to come right out and tell him.

As she looked at the heart-shaped cards she had a sudden flash of inspiration. *I'll wear the locket to Ellen's party*, she thought. *It'll be like a private Valentine message. He can't help but know how I feel then.*

She felt a sharp dig in her ribs. "There's Ken over by the soda fountain," Amy whispered urgently. "What should I do?"

"Go talk to him," Elizabeth said.

"Come with me," Amy begged. "I'm afraid I'll do something stupid."

"Amy," Elizabeth said, "if you're trying to get him to ask you out, it's probably not a great idea to have me tagging along."

Before Amy could respond, Ken turned around and caught sight of her. His jaw dropped for a moment. Then he began to laugh hysterically.

"Oh, no," Amy groaned. "I *do* look stupid. I never should have trusted Lila and Kimberly."

Ken came over and clapped Amy on the back. "You've really got a great sense of humor, Amy. Who else would get dressed up for Halloween around Valentine's Day? That's a great gag. It really tells people how you feel about all this silly romantic stuff." He snorted. "Look over there at Peter De-Haven."

Peter was talking to Melissa while trying to conceal a huge heart-shaped box of candy behind his back. Melissa was carefully pretending not to see it.

Ken shook his head and laughed. "Can you believe it? Everybody's acting totally ridiculous." He patted Amy on the shoulder. "Good thing you and I have more sense. Well, I've got to go and give Peter a hard time." He looked at the peace sign on

Amy's cheek and started laughing again. "You crack me up." Then he hurried away.

Amy watched him go, looking dejected. "Now what?" she asked sadly. "Ken doesn't think I'm pretty. He thinks I'm a big joke."

"Oh, Amy, no he doesn't," Elizabeth said consolingly, leading her friend over to the soda fountain. "I really think he likes you. He just doesn't know how to show it."

"Thanks, Elizabeth," Amy said as they sat down. "But it's pretty obvious that Ken isn't going to ask me to Ellen's party. Should I stay home or just go without a date?"

"I wish I could go without a date," Elizabeth commented. "It would sure make things easier."

"Make what things easier?" Amy asked.

Elizabeth dropped her voice to a whisper. "I'm pretty sure that Jessica still likes Aaron and that he still likes her. I've been working on a plan to get them back together."

Amy raised her eyebrows. "But if Jessica and Aaron get back together, doesn't that sort of leave you out in the cold?" she asked.

"I've been working on a plan to fix that, too," Elizabeth said.

"You mean you're going to try to get Todd back?" Amy asked eagerly. "That's great! You two really belong together." She paused. "But how? It looks as though he's really in Veronica's clutches."

Elizabeth smiled and lifted one eyebrow. "If

you were in Veronica's clutches, you'd probably be wanting out by now, wouldn't you?"

"Absolutely," Amy agreed.

"So why isn't he out?" Elizabeth asked.

"Probably because everybody's so couples-crazy right now. Todd doesn't want to be without a girlfriend. Plus he thinks you're mad at him," she answered.

"Right," Elizabeth said. "So I've got to let him know I'm not mad at him anymore. You know the locket he gave me the night of the dance?"

Amy nodded.

"I'm going to wear it to Ellen's party," Elizabeth said. "When Todd sees it, he'll know how I feel. It'll be like a secret message."

"Maybe it's too secret," Amy commented skeptically. "He might not catch on. Why don't you just tell him how you feel?"

"Why don't *you* just tell *Ken* how you feel?" Elizabeth asked.

"OK, OK, I see your point."

"Besides, think how much more romantic it is this way," Elizabeth whispered. She smiled as she began to imagine the night of the party. Todd would look over in her direction, see the locket, and immediately turn away from Veronica. The music would swell and Todd would run toward her in slow motion. "Elizabeth!" he would cry. "Elizabeth!"

"Elizabeth!" Amy's voice said.

Elizabeth woke from her daydream with a start.

"Elizabeth," Amy said again impatiently. "Are you OK?"

"Sorry," Elizabeth said quickly. "I was just daydreaming."

"About Todd?" Amy asked with a grin.

"I'm afraid so," Elizabeth admitted.

Amy snorted. "Ken is right. This romance stuff is making everybody act totally weird. Here you are in the drugstore, staring off into space like a zombie. And I look like I just got back from a peace rally or something. We've got to get a grip. We used to be perfectly sane and sensible people. And now," Amy exclaimed, her voice rising in frustration, "we're acting like total lunatics!"

Just then Ken reappeared at Amy's side and tapped her on the shoulder.

"Aaah!" Amy shrieked, startled.

Ken took a wary step back, and Elizabeth had to bite her lip to keep from laughing. Amy stared at Ken, so surprised by his sudden appearance that she couldn't say a word.

Ken cleared his throat. "I've been thinking," he said, nervously kicking the bottom of Amy's stool. "We probably ought to plan on going to Ellen's party together. That way, neither of us has to worry about getting a date." He gave Peter a contemptuous look. "You sure won't catch me asking some girl out," he said. Then he turned and hurried away.

Amy turned toward Elizabeth and shook her head in confusion. "If I'm not a girl, what am I? Chopped liver?"

Eleven

It was Friday night and the Wakefields were having dinner early so that the girls could get ready for Ellen's party. So far it had been a very quiet meal. Elizabeth couldn't help thinking how different this night was from the last time they had gotten ready for a party.

Before the school dance, Elizabeth had felt excited and giddy, certain that the evening was going to be a success. She and Jessica had chattered happily all through dinner.

But now Elizabeth felt too anxious and nervous to talk. Jessica was unusually quiet, too.

"How come all your little friends aren't over here getting dressed?" Steven asked, reaching for another roll. "Won't Mom and Dad's disaster insurance cover another pre-date party?"

Elizabeth laughed in spite of herself, and so did Jessica. Their eyes met across the table and they exchanged looks—just like in the old days. Elizabeth suddenly felt happier. *If everything goes according to plan*, she thought, *maybe Jessica and I will be friends again later tonight.*

"Some of the Unicorns did want to come over," Jessica answered. "But I thought it might get too noisy."

"We wouldn't have minded," Mrs. Wakefield said. "It was fun having all you girls here last time. You know we're always happy to have your friends over."

Jessica shrugged. "I know. I guess maybe I just didn't feel like having all of them over this time."

She didn't want to have her friends over because she's not in the mood to laugh and have fun, thought Elizabeth. *And that's because she's feeling miserable over Aaron.*

Elizabeth looked down at her plate to hide her smile. With any luck, Jessica and Aaron would be reunited by the end of the evening.

"What about you, Elizabeth?" her mother asked. "Will Melissa and Amy be coming over to get dressed with you?"

Elizabeth shook her head. "No. I didn't feel like having my friends over this time, either." *I've got too much to do,* she thought.

"Will the boys be coming here to pick you up?" Mr. Wakefield asked.

"No!" Elizabeth and Jessica said together.

"I'm meeting Aaron there," Elizabeth said quickly. "I was hoping you would drive me to the party. If you can't, I can walk. It's not far."

"I'm supposed to meet Bruce, too," Jessica said.

"I'll be happy to drive both of you," Mr. Wakefield replied. "What time will you be ready to leave?"

"I'll be ready whenever Jessica wants to go," Elizabeth said quickly.

"Well," Jessica hedged, "what time do you think you'll be dressed and ready?"

"Whatever time you want," Elizabeth said.

"It's up to you," Jessica said.

"I don't want to hurry you," Elizabeth replied politely.

Mr. Wakefield raised his eyebrows. "Well, I'm at your service, whatever you decide. Just let me know."

Jessica put down her knife and fork.

"Are you getting dressed now?" Elizabeth asked eagerly.

"Are you?" Jessica asked.

"I guess I am if you are," Elizabeth replied.

"Just go already," exclaimed Steven in frustration. He looked at his parents and shook his head. "I don't know which is worse—listening to them be rude to each other, or listening to them be polite to each other."

"Leave your sisters alone and finish your dinner," Mrs. Wakefield said firmly.

The two girls exchanged another amused look and hurried upstairs.

Thirty minutes later, Elizabeth had washed her hair, blown it dry, and dabbed on a little lipstick and mascara. Jessica had been in and out of the bathroom several times, too. When Elizabeth had last seen her, five minutes earlier, she was still in her underwear.

Elizabeth was wearing only her underwear, too. She sat down on the edge of her bed and sighed. *Hurry up and get dressed,* she urged her sister mentally. She needed to know what Jessica was planning to wear before she got dressed herself.

I can at least put on my locket, Elizabeth thought. She went over to her night table to find the locket. As she looked for it she smiled, imagining how Todd would feel when he saw it. Todd was pretty perceptive. She was sure he'd get the message.

But even after Elizabeth had searched all over, the locket was nowhere to be found. *I wonder if Jessica knows anything about it. I'll go in and ask her. It'll give me a good excuse to see what she's wearing.*

Elizabeth went through the bathroom and knocked on Jessica's door.

"Come in," Jessica called out quickly.

Elizabeth stepped inside and her eyes widened. She couldn't believe it. Jessica was *still* in her underwear. She hoped this wasn't going to be one of those occasions when Jessica changed clothes fifty times. They'd be there until midnight.

"The party is tonight, you know," Elizabeth said. "How long are you going to take to decide what to wear?"

"Look who's talking," Jessica retorted. "You're not dressed, either."

Elizabeth smiled weakly and shrugged. She couldn't exactly tell her sister that she couldn't get dressed until she saw what Jessica was wearing. "Have you seen my locket?" she asked.

"What locket?" Jessica asked distractedly.

Elizabeth sighed. "Never mind." It was obvious that Jessica didn't know anything about it. Elizabeth went back to her own room and looked around. *Where is it?* she wondered in frustration. She got down on her hands and knees and looked under the night table. Then she crawled across the floor, looking under every piece of furniture. *This is impossible. It has to be here somewhere.*

Then she had a terrible thought. Her mother had vacuumed the house on Tuesday. The locket must have fallen on the floor and been sucked up into the vacuum cleaner. She didn't have time to take the vacuum cleaner bag apart before she left. She would just have to go to the party without the locket. Elizabeth was so disappointed that she felt like crying.

Behind her, she heard a creak. She turned and saw Jessica peeping at her from the hall. "What?" Elizabeth asked irritatedly.

Jessica looked startled to have been caught. Then her own face darkened with annoyance. "What are you doing crawling around on the floor?" she demanded.

"What are you doing asking me questions when you're supposed to be getting dressed?" Elizabeth snapped.

"I . . . uh . . . thought I heard you call me," Jessica said. "I guess I was hearing things." Then she shut the door.

Elizabeth sat back on her heels. *Jessica sure is acting strange*, she thought.

Then she turned her attention back to the locket problem. It just wasn't in the room. That meant she probably wouldn't make much progress with Todd that night. *Oh well*, she thought with a sigh, *I guess I'll just have to concentrate on helping Jessica this time.*

Ten minutes later, Jessica was sitting on her bed, still in her underwear. *What's wrong with Elizabeth?* she thought with irritation. *She's usually dressed in about five minutes.*

She waited another minute and then decided

to try again. She had to find out what Elizabeth was planning to wear.

Jessica went through the connecting bathroom and knocked on Elizabeth's door. *I hope she's not wearing that gross blue sweater with the lace collar*, she thought. *I wouldn't want to have to wear that to a party —even if it is for a good cause.*

"Come in," Elizabeth called out eagerly.

Jessica walked in and stared at her sister in consternation.

Elizabeth stared back, looking equally dismayed.

"You're not dressed yet!" they both exclaimed in an accusing tone.

"I'm . . . uh . . . still trying to decide what to wear," Jessica explained.

"Me too," Elizabeth said quickly.

Darn! Jessica thought. "OK, then. I'll get lost and let you get dressed."

Jessica hurried toward the door.

"By the way, Jess, what did you want?" Elizabeth asked. "You came in here for something."

Jessica turned. "Oh, yeah. I, um, wanted to borrow your lip liner."

"I don't have any."

"OK," Jessica said, ducking back into the bathroom. She closed the door and stood there for a moment with a frown on her face. Then she went over and turned on the tap so it would sound as if she was at the sink. She picked up the glass that held their toothpaste and toothbrushes and rattled it to give the impression that she was busy getting ready. Then she tiptoed back to the door that led to Elizabeth's room.

Very cautiously, she opened the door a crack and peered in. To her surprise, Elizabeth's room was empty. Jessica sighed. This was a lot harder than she had anticipated.

She closed the door to Elizabeth's room and turned off the tap. When she stepped back into her own room, she jumped in surprise. Elizabeth was looking furtively into her room from the hallway.

"What are you doing?" Jessica demanded.

Elizabeth seemed confused for a moment. Finally she said slowly, "I just wanted to know if you had any . . . uh . . . hairbands," Elizabeth said.

"Here," Jessica said, grabbing a handful of hairbands from her night table. She handed them to Elizabeth. "Now get dressed," she said. "I don't want to be late."

Elizabeth took the hairbands and disappeared.

Elizabeth paced around her room impatiently. *Why does Jessica always have to take so long to get ready? I'll sneak through the bathroom and take another look.*

She carefully opened the door to the bathroom. Then she slowly stepped inside—and found herself face to face with Jessica!

"Aren't you dressed yet?" Jessica exclaimed,

glaring at Elizabeth. Elizabeth tried frantically to think of another excuse. "I was just . . ." Elizabeth glanced around the bathroom and noticed her denim skirt hanging on a hook. ". . . looking for my denim skirt," she finished. "There it is."

"You're wearing that?" Jessica asked eagerly.

Elizabeth sighed. She was stuck now. "Yes," she answered.

Jessica bit her lip. "You know, I was thinking of wearing my denim miniskirt, too."

"Oh, really?" Elizabeth said. This was good news.

"If we wear different tops, it won't make any difference, right?" Jessica said.

"Right," Elizabeth agreed encouragingly.

"Good," Jessica said. She turned and hurried out of the bathroom.

It's about time, Jessica thought as she rummaged through her closet in search of her own denim miniskirt. Things were going to be tricky, but she was pretty sure she could pull it off.

For once she didn't spend much time getting ready. She pulled a plain blue blouse out of her closet and decided not to curl her hair. She didn't really want people to pay much attention to her that night.

She heard the door to Elizabeth's room open. Jessica quickly finished buttoning up her blouse and hurried to her own door. She opened it and looked out at Elizabeth. "Ready?" Jessica asked, noting Elizabeth's pink sweater.

"Ready," Elizabeth said.

"I'll be right there." Jessica shut her door quickly and hurried to her closet. She had a pink sweater almost exactly like the one Elizabeth was wearing. When she found it, she stuffed it down into the bottom of her large purse.

She rushed back out to the hall, but Elizabeth was gone. Jessica figured that she must already have gone downstairs. But just then the door to Elizabeth's room opened and she came out. "Let's party," she said with a grin.

Jessica was startled. *Wow, Elizabeth sounds just like me.*

Twelve

"Oh, good grief," Ken said in a disgusted voice. "Look at this stuff. We know it's Valentine's Day. They don't have to rub it in."

But Amy's eyes sparkled as she looked around the Ritemans' spacious home. It looked like a Valentine wonderland. Heart-shaped helium balloons were clustered everywhere. Hundreds of Valentine cards were arranged on tables and stuck in mirrors —everything from old-fashioned Victorian cards with cherubs and flowery poems to gag Valentines with insulting things written on them.

"I think it looks wonderful," Amy exclaimed as she and Ken headed for the refreshments.

"Oh, no," Ken moaned, peering into the large

crystal punch bowl. "They've ruined perfectly good punch with heart-shaped ice cubes."

"Look at all this great food," Amy said, deciding to ignore Ken's unromantic attitude. The table was laden with heart-shaped cupcakes, pink and red frosted cookies, and little pink heart-shaped mints with silly messages written on them.

Ellen's parents had wired the sound system so that music was playing both in the living room and out on the glassed-in patio. The furniture in both rooms had been pushed against the walls, and lots of couples were already dancing.

"It looks like just about every kid from Sweet Valley Middle School is here," Ken commented sourly. "Look, there's even a big crowd out in the backyard."

"Look at the little heart-shaped lanterns around the pool," Amy said, pointing.

"Those can be a real fire hazard if you're not careful," Ken said seriously.

How can Ken be so completely immune to this romantic atmosphere? Amy wondered. She looked around at the dancing couples and the decorations. *Maybe he'll feel differently after we've spent a little more time together.*

"Hi, Amy. Hi, Ken," Ellen said, coming over to join them. "Thanks for coming."

"Thanks for inviting us," Amy said. "Everything looks great. It must have been a lot of work."

"It was," Ellen said. "But my parents did most

of it. They got so carried away by the whole thing, you would have thought it was their party." She laughed. "The heart-shaped balloons were my dad's idea. You don't think they're too much, do you?"

"No!" Ken replied quickly.

Amy gave him a surprised look.

"I like the balloons," Ken said, looking up at the ceiling.

"They are pretty romantic," Ellen agreed with a knowing smile.

"That's not why I like them," Ken said hurriedly, looking embarrassed. "They're colorful, that's all. Come on, Amy. Let's try some of those cookies."

Ken took Amy's arm and practically dragged her toward a plate of cookies at the other end of the table. He threw a nervous glance over his shoulder at Ellen. "Boy, am I glad you're not one of those Unicorns," he said darkly. "You've got to watch yourself every minute around them."

"What do you mean?" Amy asked.

Ken rolled his eyes. "They're all obsessed with this romance stuff. It's like they're always trying to get guys to say mushy things." He grinned at Amy and playfully punched her arm. "That's why I like hanging out with you, Amy. You never do stuff like that. It's almost like being with another guy."

Oh, great! Amy thought ruefully. *Just what I wanted to hear.*

Ken gave her another look and smiled. "By the way, you look really nice tonight," he said.

"Really?" Amy smiled back at him. Kimberly and Lila had offered to help her put together an outfit for the party, but Amy had told them no thanks. She was afraid she might wind up dressed like an astronaut or a cowboy or something. She had decided to wear something that she liked and felt comfortable in. It was nice to know that Ken appreciated her taste.

She looked down at her gray stirrup pants and matching tunic top. "You like this outfit, huh?" she said, hoping to prompt another compliment.

Ken looked her up and down and nodded. "Yeah, I really do. It reminds me of my baseball uniform."

"Oh," Amy said, her face falling.

But Ken didn't notice. He had just thrown a mint high in the air, opened his mouth wide, and turned his face upward. The mint fell neatly into his mouth and he lifted his arms. "Two points!" he yelled happily.

Ken, you're soooo romantic, Amy thought sourly.

"Hi, guys," Todd said, coming over to join them.

Veronica was right beside him. When she saw Amy, she squeezed Todd's arm possessively and smirked.

Yuck, Amy thought. *How can Todd stand her?*

"Where's your little buddy Elizabeth?" Veronica asked Amy. "Isn't she coming? It would be terrible for her to miss such a nice party, wouldn't it, Todd?"

"Sure," Todd mumbled. "I guess so."

"She'll be here," Amy said, giving Veronica a level stare. *And when she gets here, I hope she wipes that smug look right off your face*, she added to herself.

As Amy watched Todd she began to think that Elizabeth's locket idea was a good one. Todd didn't look very happy. When he saw Elizabeth wearing his locket, he would probably be so thrilled that he'd dump Veronica right away.

Just then Veronica reached back and ran her hand through her silky dark hair. As she did, the neck of her sweater shifted a little, and Amy gasped. Veronica was wearing a locket just like Elizabeth's!

Amy gazed at Todd in surprise. What a jerk! Was he going to hand out lockets to every girl at school?

Todd smiled at Amy. "These cookies look really good," he said, reaching toward the tray. "Want one?"

Amy felt so furious that she could hardly see straight. How dare Todd smile at her and offer her a cookie when he knew she was Elizabeth's best friend? How could he have given Elizabeth's enemy a locket just like the one he'd given Elizabeth?

And how dare Ken stand there chewing mints as though he had no idea what was going on?

"No," Amy snapped. "I don't want a cookie." She turned on her heel and stalked off. She marched out of the room, across the patio, and out the door to the backyard.

"Amy?" Ken called, hurrying after her. "Hey, Amy, wait up! What's the matter? You sounded really mad at Todd back there."

"I think boys *stink!*" Amy shouted angrily, whirling around to face him. "I think Aaron stinks. I think Bruce stinks. I think Todd stinks. And I think *you* stink most of all!"

Ken looked taken aback. "Geez, Amy, what did I do?"

"You . . . you . . . you . . ." How could she possibly explain? "You said the heart-shaped lanterns were a fire hazard! You are so unbelievably dense that there's no point in talking to you."

"Please don't be mad," Ken said. "I'm sorry I said the lanterns were a fire hazard. That was a stupid thing to say."

Amy gave him a long look. Was she being too hard on him?

Ken took her hand and squeezed it. "No wonder you were mad. You're right. I *was* being completely dense."

Amy's heart began to flutter. Maybe he really was beginning to understand.

"Sometimes it takes a smart girl like you to straighten out a dumb guy like me."

Ken was amazingly sweet when he apologized, Amy decided. How could she have thought he wasn't romantic? This was probably the most romantic moment of her whole life.

He smacked his hand against his forehead. "Why didn't I see it right away? It's so obvious."

Amy blushed. It really was obvious. They were perfect for each other. But Amy didn't want to make Ken feel bad. "It took me a while to see it, too," she said soothingly.

"You're just trying to make me feel better," Ken said. "I mean, how can they be a fire hazard when they're around the swimming pool? Water can't catch on fire."

Amy's mouth dropped open. Her eyes bulged. Ken Matthews was a total *nincompoop*!

"Hey, listen," he said. "They're playing music outside now. Come on, let's dance over by the pool." He took her hand and dragged her toward the swimming pool. The next thing Amy knew, she and Ken were dancing with a lot of other couples by the light of the flickering heart-shaped lanterns.

Amy sighed. *Oh well*, she thought. *Ken Matthews might be a nincompoop, but he's still cute.*

Ken looked around and then smiled at Amy. "You know," he said thoughtfully, "these lanterns really are pretty."

"I guess so," Amy replied, no longer caring much.

"And so are you," Ken added shyly.

"Where have you guys been?" Ellen demanded when she opened the door for Elizabeth and Jessica.

Elizabeth opened her mouth to apologize, but Ellen didn't give her a chance to speak. "Never mind. I'm sure Jessica had to change clothes a million times before she decided what to wear. Come on in."

The twins stepped inside. They both gasped when they saw the gorgeous decorations.

"Your house looks great," Jessica cried.

"Elizabeth," Aaron said, rushing over. "I've been waiting for you. Come on, let's dance."

Aaron didn't even look at Jessica. But Elizabeth had the feeling that he had to make an effort not to.

He took Elizabeth's arm and steered her toward the patio. "I've been waiting for you for an hour," he said. "We've got a lot of dancing to catch up on."

Two seconds later, Elizabeth and Aaron were in the middle of a crowd of dancing couples on the patio.

A new song began to play and Aaron moved his shoulders to the beat. "You got here just in time. This is my favorite song."

Elizabeth smiled. "I like this song, too. But I'll

be able to dance better without my purse. I'm going to go put it in one of the bedrooms."

She started to hurry away, but Aaron grabbed the purse out of her hands and shoved it under a chair. "It'll be OK there," he said. Before she could protest, he took her by the hand and twirled her around. "You were so late, I was afraid we'd *never* get to dance."

Uh-oh, Elizabeth thought. *It's not going to be so easy to get away from Aaron tonight.*

Jessica cornered Veronica in the living room. "You told me you were changing just a few answers," she hissed. "Mandy told me Elizabeth got an F on her homework."

"So?" Veronica said, sounding bored. Then she smiled. "I'm so glad Elizabeth is finally here. I'm looking forward to teasing her a little about that F."

"You say one word and I'll tell her what you did," Jessica threatened.

Veronica narrowed her eyes and took a step toward Jessica. "If you tell on me, Jessica, I'll do to you what I did to Elizabeth."

"Hah," Jessica replied. "I wouldn't let you near my homework."

A little smile appeared at the corners of Veronica's mouth. "That's not what I mean," she said.

Jessica blinked in confusion. "What *do* you mean?" she asked.

Veronica jerked her head toward Bruce, who

was standing over by the stereo system, flipping through the CDs. "I could take Bruce away from you—just like I took Todd away from Elizabeth." She smirked. "It would really be something to have those two fighting over me. People would think I was the most popular girl at Sweet Valley Middle School."

Jessica tossed her head. "You couldn't even if you tried," she challenged.

Veronica lifted one eyebrow. "Sure I could."

"Well, I'll believe it when I see it," Jessica said haughtily, turning away. She walked over to Bruce, hoping with all her might that Veronica would follow through on her threat. "Hi, Bruce," she said with a smile.

Bruce frowned. "Where have you been?" he demanded. "I'm not used to having girls keep me waiting."

Jessica sighed. She didn't know how much longer she could stand Bruce's humongous ego. "Sorry," she said, trying to come up with a believable story. "We had to wait for my father to drive us. Just before we left, he got a phone call and—"

As usual, Bruce didn't let her finish her sentence. "You know, I don't usually go to parties given by sixth graders." He glanced at his reflection in the glass door of the stereo cabinet and ran a hand through his hair. "But I know how important it is to you to be seen with me. So I decided to make an exception."

He looked at Jessica and turned his head back and forth. "So what do you think?" he asked with an expectant grin.

"What do I think about what?" Jessica asked.

"Don't you notice anything different?" Bruce asked her in disbelief.

"I don't think so," Jessica replied.

Bruce looked annoyed. "Come on, Jessica. Think! Pay attention!"

Jessica shrugged. She didn't have the slightest idea what he was talking about.

"My hair!" Bruce cried, pointing to his head with both forefingers. "My hair! It's parted on the left. I usually part it on the right. How could you not notice? I mean, it's so obvious. It makes a big difference in the way I look."

"*I* noticed it right away," said a smooth voice at Jessica's elbow. Jessica turned and saw Veronica standing by her side, smiling at Bruce.

"You did?" Bruce said. "Really?" He looked at Jessica and winked. Then he turned to face Veronica. "Think it makes me look more like somebody famous?" he asked. "People keep telling me I look like somebody really famous. Who do I look like? Come on. Let's see if you're up on your rock stars."

Veronica studied Bruce. "Of course! You look just like . . . um . . . Donny Diamond."

Bruce's face fell and Veronica quickly corrected herself. "Not Donny Diamond. That's not his name. It's that other guy . . ."

Bruce's lips were unconsciously forming a *j* sound. Veronica waved her hands in frustration. "Oh, it's right on the tip of my tongue. It's that guy whose name starts with a *J.* You look exactly like him. It's Jack . . . Jim . . . John . . . Johnny?"

Bruce was nodding now.

"Johnny Buck!" Veronica cried. "Of course. That's who you look like."

Just then the other Unicorns walked up. "Who looks like Johnny Buck?" Lila asked.

"Bruce," Veronica answered. "He looks exactly like Johnny Buck, doesn't he?"

Bruce struck a pose and played a little air guitar. "It's Johnny Buck!" he shouted. "Live from the Riteman living room."

All the girls giggled and applauded. Jessica rolled her eyes and wondered if she was going to be sick. She glanced over and saw Todd standing by the refreshment table.

"You know, I've always thought Bruce looked more like a movie star than a rock star," Tamara said breathlessly.

"Really?" Bruce asked. "Which one?"

"The guy who was in *Last Date of the Summer*," Tamara answered.

"You mean David Wall?" Lila said.

"No," Kimberly argued. "He looks more like the guy who was in *Dreaming of You*."

Betsy Gordon elbowed her way into the group.

"That's who he looks like," she confirmed. "The guy in *Dreaming of You*."

Little by little, Jessica allowed herself to be edged out of the group of girls who were giggling around Bruce. She smiled inwardly as she saw that Veronica was standing as close to Bruce as she possibly could.

She thinks she's teaching me a lesson, Jessica thought. *But she doesn't know she's really doing me a big favor. Me and Elizabeth both.*

Jessica threw one last look over her shoulder to make sure that Bruce hadn't noticed her disappearance. Then she grabbed her purse and hurried toward the bathroom in the laundry room off the kitchen.

She slipped inside and locked the door behind her. It didn't take her long to change out of her blue blouse and into the pink sweater. As she combed her hair into a ponytail she forced her face into a serious and shy expression. "Hi, Todd," she said softly, doing her best to imitate her sister.

Come on! Elizabeth thought impatiently. She had been standing outside the downstairs bathroom for five minutes. Whoever was in there was sure taking a long time. Elizabeth was afraid Aaron would come looking for her if she didn't get back out to the patio soon. It hadn't been easy to get away. Aaron was a real party animal.

I'd better find another bathroom upstairs, Elizabeth

decided. She hurried up the stairs and found one on the upstairs landing. She ducked inside and fished a plain blue blouse out of her purse.

In less than two minutes she had completed her transformation. She tossed her head and tried out a flirtatious look in the mirror. "Hi, Aaron," she said with a big smile, doing her best to look and sound like Jessica. Then she took a deep breath, opened the bathroom door, and headed off to find Aaron.

Thirteen

◇

"Hi, Todd. Having a good time?"

When Todd looked up and saw someone he thought was Elizabeth standing next to him, he jumped in surprise and almost choked on the mint he was eating.

He began to cough and Jessica pounded him on the back. "Sorry if I scared you," she said in Elizabeth's sweetest voice.

Todd managed to catch his breath. "You didn't *scare* me." He took a big gulp of soda. "You just surprised me. I mean, I thought you weren't speaking to me."

"I wasn't," Jessica said. "But then I realized I was being really silly. We're old friends, right?"

"Sure," Todd said, doing his best to look cool

and unconcerned. He leaned back casually against the wall, but it was farther away than he realized.

"Whoa!" he cried as he began to fall.

Quick as lightning, Jessica reached out and caught Todd by the lapels of his shirt. "Watch it," she said, briskly hoisting him to his feet.

Todd's face was beet red. He hastily brushed himself off. "Uh . . . thanks," he stammered. "I don't know what happened there. I just sort of lost my balance for a minute."

Jessica smiled inwardly. There was no longer any doubt in her mind that Todd still liked Elizabeth. How else could a person possibly be so nervous and klutzy?

"It could happen to anyone," Jessica said, trying to make her voice sound really understanding. "In fact, it's even happened to me once or twice." Jessica did her best to giggle like Elizabeth as she patted the collar of Todd's shirt back into shape.

"So, Todd . . ." she said.

Todd looked at her gravely. Jessica knew this was going to be tough. He was pretty intelligent. And so was Elizabeth. Jessica bit her lip. She needed to think of something intelligent to talk about.

"So, Todd," she began again, "read any good books lately?"

"Hi, Aaron," Elizabeth said, giving Aaron a dazzling smile.

Aaron automatically smiled back. "Hi," he said happily. Then his face clouded over as he remembered that he and Jessica weren't speaking. "See you later," he mumbled, turning to walk away.

Normally, Elizabeth would have been humiliated by such a pointed rejection. *You're not Elizabeth,* she reminded herself. *You're Jessica. Be more aggressive.*

"Don't run away," she said quickly. "I was hoping maybe we could dance."

Aaron frowned. "Elizabeth is my date," he reminded her. "And Bruce Patman is yours," he added angrily. "Last time you dumped me to dance with Bruce. This time you're dumping Bruce to dance with me. What are you trying to do, anyway? Be the date-dumping champion of Sweet Valley?"

Aaron sounded really angry. But Elizabeth knew he was angry because his feelings were hurt.

Elizabeth loved and admired Jessica. But she was glad that it was she and not her sister who was having this conversation with Aaron. Jessica wasn't always as perceptive as Elizabeth. She might not have realized that Aaron's anger came from hurt feelings. Her response would probably be to get angry herself. Then she would say something even more hurtful and the situation would get worse.

Jessica may have more spunk than I do, thought Elizabeth. *But I have more tact. And this is definitely a situation that calls for tact.*

"Gosh, Aaron," Elizabeth said, "I'm sorry you

think that. I wasn't trying to do anything that would hurt your feelings. I saw you over here by yourself and thought it would be a good opportunity for us to talk—and maybe be friends again."

Aaron looked ashamed. "I'm sorry," he muttered. "I guess I sounded a little harsh."

"That's OK," Elizabeth assured him. "I don't blame you. The last few days have been kind of rough."

"What do you mean, rough?" he asked quickly. "Rough on who? Not me. Elizabeth is a great girl. I really like being with her. So don't say anything bad about her."

"Of course Elizabeth is a great girl," Elizabeth said. "And because she's so great, she wants you to be happy. She's a great sister, too. And that means she wants me to be happy."

"Uh-huh." Aaron frowned with the effort of trying to follow her reasoning. "So?"

"Are you happy, Aaron?" Elizabeth asked, looking soulfully into his eyes.

"Sure. I guess so. Why not? I mean, I hadn't really thought about it." He stared back at her. "But now that you ask, maybe I'm not as happy as I used to be," he admitted softly.

"I'm not as happy as I used to be, either," Elizabeth said bluntly.

"Really?" Aaron stared at her warily. He still didn't seem completely sure whether or not to trust her. "Why not?" he asked suspiciously.

Elizabeth touched his arm. "Probably for the same reason you're not happy. And I don't think Elizabeth is happy, either."

"You don't?" Aaron asked.

Elizabeth shook her head. "No. That's probably why she did so poorly on her math homework."

Aaron shook his head sadly. "Yeah, I sort of wondered about that myself. You think it's because of me, huh? Because she doesn't really like me?"

"It's not that I—that she doesn't like you," Elizabeth said. *Careful,* she told herself. "It's probably because she still likes Todd. Just like I still like you," she added boldly.

"Wow," Aaron said. He gave a low whistle. "You still like me? This is really sort of a big mess, isn't it?"

There was a burst of laughter from the other side of the room, and they both looked over to see Bruce surrounded by adoring Unicorns. The sight seemed to remind Aaron of what had started the big mess.

He scowled at Jessica. "If you like me so much, how come you left me standing all alone at the dance and went off with Bruce?"

Good question, Elizabeth thought. But she was prepared for it. "You know how carried away I get with things. Being asked to dance by a seventh grader is every sixth-grade girl's dream. If some girl in the seventh grade paid a lot of attention to you, wouldn't it turn *your* head?"

Aaron looked thoughtful. "Yeah, I guess it would. So I suppose I can't really blame you." He scowled again. "But did you have to kiss him?"

Elizabeth sighed. "Let me see if I can explain about that."

"You dance really well," Ken said with a smile.

"Thanks." Amy smiled back. But she was having a hard time concentrating on her dancing. She was too busy trying to see what was going on inside the patio.

Wouldn't you know? she thought sourly. *I finally get Ken interested and I can't even enjoy myself because I'm too busy worrying about Elizabeth's love life.*

"I'm really thirsty," she said. "I think I'll get some soda. Want me to get you some?"

"No, let me get it," Ken offered. He smiled. "After all, I am your date."

Amy smiled back. "Thanks. That would be terrific." Once Ken was out of the way, she figured, she would be able to warn Elizabeth to call off her campaign to get Todd back. Judging from the locket around Veronica's neck, Todd didn't want to be gotten back. Amy had to stop Elizabeth before she made a fool of herself.

She watched Ken disappear into the house. Then she headed for the patio door.

* * *

"So anyway," Todd said, "the best part of the book was the ending, where the count gets his revenge and . . ."

Jessica smiled and opened her eyes very wide, trying to look interested. She tightened her jaw to stifle another yawn. Todd had just told her the entire plot of the book he had just read. It was a very long and complicated story, and Jessica was starting to feel a little sleepy.

Was this really the kind of stuff Todd and Elizabeth talked about? How incredibly boring! Maybe she wasn't doing Elizabeth such a big favor by getting her back together with Todd.

"It was really exciting," Todd went on. "It was almost as good as the other book I read last week."

"The *other* book?" Jessica said, stunned. "You read *two* books last week? For fun?" *Get a life*, she thought. Then she remembered that she was supposed to be Elizabeth. "I mean, that's great," she said. "I can't believe you read two whole books."

As soon as it was out of her mouth she knew it was the wrong thing to say.

"What's the big deal?" Todd asked impatiently. "You read at least two books almost every week." Then a disgusted look crossed his face and he rolled his eyes. "Oh, I get it. You're doing the kind of stuff Jessica does. Pretending to be really impressed with a guy to build up his ego and make him like you."

"Jessica doesn't do that kind of thing," Jessica retorted.

Todd looked skeptical. "Yes, she does. Rick Hunter told me all about it."

Jessica began to blush furiously. Actually, she knew that she sometimes *did* do that kind of thing. But it was pretty embarrassing to realize that Rick Hunter was making fun of her for doing it.

"OK," she admitted grudgingly. "Maybe she does, just a little. But Eliz—but *I* don't," she corrected herself quickly.

She was beginning to get a little rattled. The twins had changed places lots of times, but this was the first time Jessica had tried to fool a boyfriend. It was more nerve-wracking than she had expected.

She smiled weakly. "I'm just so glad to hear that you still like to read," she explained. "I thought you might have changed. But you haven't," she babbled nervously. "You still love to read. I love to read. We both love to read. That's why we have so much in common. And since we do have all this stuff in common, I really think we should be friends again."

Jessica batted her eyelashes—just a little. "Don't you think we should be friends again?" she continued in a coaxing tone. It wasn't really Elizabeth's style, but Jessica just couldn't help herself. Besides, she figured it wouldn't hurt Elizabeth to try a little eyelash-batting once in a while.

Todd snorted and batted his eyelashes back at

her. "I *used* to think so. Now I'm not so sure." He looked at his watch. "Geez, I've spent almost ten minutes yakking about books."

Only ten minutes? Jessica thought in amazement. It had seemed more like an hour to her.

"I'd better find my date," Todd said. "I don't want to be rude." He started to walk away, but Jessica grabbed his sleeve and yanked him back.

"Veronica's busy talking to Bruce," she said. "Don't worry about her."

Todd looked startled at Elizabeth's sudden aggressiveness. "You're the one who's changed, Elizabeth," he suddenly burst out. "And not for the better, either."

"How have I changed?" Jessica demanded.

"Veronica told me what you did," he said. "At first I had a lot of trouble believing you would do something like that, but—"

"What did I do?"

"Hey," said a sharp voice behind Jessica. "Why don't you quit bothering my date?"

Jessica whirled around and saw Veronica giving her a dirty look. Jessica put her hands on her hips. "Do you mind? We're trying to have a private conversation here."

"As a matter of fact," Veronica purred, "I do mind. Todd is my date." She took Todd's arm and looked at him. "And I'd like to dance now."

"Why don't you dance with Bruce Patman?"

Jessica sneered. "You sure seemed to think he was fascinating a few minutes ago."

Todd gasped. "Elizabeth! Don't talk to Veronica that way."

Jessica's heart sank. Elizabeth would never behave this way. Jessica was afraid she had just blown things permanently between Todd and her sister. This whole scheme had been a terrible mistake.

"Pssst! Pssst!" an insistent voice hissed behind her.

Jessica turned and saw Amy frantically waving at her from the other side of the patio. She shook her head. Sometimes Amy Sutton was so weird. She was going to have to speak to Elizabeth about her. That made Jessica remember that she was supposed to *be* Elizabeth. "Excuse me," she said as politely as she could. "I'll be right back."

She hurried over to Amy. "What is it? I'm a little busy right now."

"I'm trying to stop you before you make a fool of yourself," Amy said urgently. "Todd really likes Veronica. No kidding. He gave her a locket just like the one he gave you. She's wearing it tonight—I saw it."

"A locket?" Jessica repeated.

Right then something clicked in her head. Elizabeth had asked her about a missing locket earlier that evening. And now, suddenly, Veronica had one. Hadn't Veronica slipped something into her pocket while she'd been snooping in Elizabeth's room? It must have been Elizabeth's locket.

Jessica whirled around, fire in her eyes. She was so angry that for a moment she forgot she was supposed to be Elizabeth. All she knew was that Veronica was the dirtiest trickster she had ever met in her whole life. And this time she wasn't going to get away with it. She stalked back over to Veronica and held out her hand.

"Hand it over," she demanded furiously.

Veronica gave her an innocent look. "What are you talking about?"

"Hand over the locket. The one you stole from Eli—from me!"

"*Stole?*" Todd exclaimed. "What are you talking about?"

Jessica pointed at the locket around Veronica's neck. "That! Veronica stole it from my room!"

Todd turned to Veronica. "You said you found it in the garbage can at school. You said you saw her throw it away after she and I broke up."

"I did," Veronica insisted.

"She did *not*," Jessica fumed. "And while we're on the subject," she said, glaring at Todd, "why is she wearing Eli—*my* locket?"

Todd flushed.

"Why shouldn't I wear it?" Veronica sneered. "*I'm* Todd's girlfriend now. Besides, you threw the locket away."

"That's not true," Jessica shouted. "You took it the day you were over at my house."

"You're a liar!" Veronica shouted back.

Todd frowned. "I've never known Elizabeth to tell a lie," he said thoughtfully. He gave Veronica a serious look. "Tell me the truth, Veronica. Did you really take it? Were you just trying to make more trouble between me and Elizabeth?"

"She *was* trying to make trouble," Jessica said.

Veronica shoved Jessica's shoulder. "Why don't you get lost and let me and Todd work this out?"

Jessica shoved Veronica back. "What makes you such a jerk, anyway?"

Veronica shoved Jessica again, a little harder. "What makes you such a goody-goody?"

"Who are you calling a goody-goody?" Jessica hissed, pushing Veronica so that she stumbled into Todd.

"Please stop it, Elizabeth," Todd begged.

"Stay out of this," snapped Veronica. She gave Jessica a hard shove that sent her hurtling backwards, across the patio, through the door, and into the living room.

Fourteen

◇

"So you never really wanted to kiss Bruce?"

"No," Elizabeth repeated for the fifteenth time. "I just couldn't get out of the way fast enough." She knew she was probably stretching the truth a little. But after all, stretching the truth was Jessica's specialty.

Aaron sighed happily. "Oh, Jessica, I can't believe how silly we've—"

But he never got to finish his sentence.

There were several surprised shouts and an outraged yelp. The crowd in the living room parted as a figure came careening through the living room as if she had been shot from a cannon.

"Yeow!" cried the figure as she tripped over a stereo speaker and sprawled at Elizabeth's feet.

Elizabeth looked down and blinked in startled surprise. Jessica stared back up at her, looking equally astonished.

Before either girl could say a word, Todd came rushing into the room. "Elizabeth! Elizabeth!" he cried out. "Are you all right?"

"Elizabeth"? thought Elizabeth as she watched Todd help her sister to her feet.

"Are you all right, Jessica?" Todd asked, turning to Elizabeth. "It looked like Elizabeth almost fell right on top of you."

"I'm fine," Elizabeth managed to squeak.

As she watched, Todd turned back toward her sister. "I'm so sorry, Elizabeth. I believe you about Veronica. I believe you about the locket. I believe you about everything. And I'm sorry I abandoned you at the dance. Can we please be friends again?"

Aaron turned to Elizabeth. "Can we be friends again, too, Jessica?"

At that moment, a romantic ballad began to play. "Let's make it up with a kiss," sang Johnny Buck over the speakers.

Elizabeth smiled at Aaron.

Jessica smiled at Todd.

Aaron grinned back at Elizabeth and leaned forward, preparing to seal the happy moment with a kiss. Todd smiled happily at Jessica and got ready to do the same. But just then, both twins spoke at once. "Excuse me," they said.

They hurried out of the living room. "This

way," Jessica said. She grabbed Elizabeth's hand and pulled her toward the bathroom in the laundry room.

Once they were inside, Jessica shut the door with a bang and both girls began to laugh hysterically.

"I can't believe you," Elizabeth exclaimed breathlessly.

"Look who's talking," Jessica gasped back.

"This proves it," Elizabeth said, unbuttoning the blue blouse and handing it to Jessica. "Great minds think alike."

"No doubt about it," Jessica said, pulling the pink sweater off over her head.

"So what's the story with my locket?"

"Veronica stole it," Jessica answered. She handed Elizabeth the pink sweater and began to put on the blue blouse. "It's a long story and I'll tell you later. We've got more important things to do right now."

"You're right," Elizabeth said, pulling on the pink sweater. She looked at her sister. "Ready?"

Jessica nodded. "Ready."

"Good." Elizabeth grinned. She pretended to play the guitar, mimicking Johnny Buck. "Let's go find Aaron and Todd and 'make it up with a kiss.' "

"Stop it!" Jessica begged. "You remind me of Bruce. And that reminds me of what an idiot I am."

Elizabeth smiled at Jessica. "I don't think

you're an idiot. I think you're a great sister. Thanks for getting me and Todd back together."

Jessica gave Elizabeth a hug. "Ditto," she said happily. "Now let's get back to the party."

Jessica opened the door and stopped short. There was a gasp in the laundry room.

The twins blinked in surprise as Ken and Amy broke apart in embarrassment. They had obviously been kissing. Ken blushed and Amy began to giggle.

"Sorry," Jessica said with a grin. "We didn't know you were out here."

"We didn't know you were in there," Amy responded. "And while we're on the subject, *why* were you in there?"

"Long story," Elizabeth and Jessica said in unison.

"I'll tell you later," Elizabeth added.

Seconds later, the two girls were back in the living room with Todd and Aaron.

"Now then." Jessica smiled at Aaron. "Where were we?"

"Just about to dance," he said softly. "To make up for the ones we missed in the gym."

Jessica smiled and put her arms around Aaron's shoulders.

Elizabeth turned toward Todd and did the same. Her heart began to thump as they swayed to the romantic music. She closed her eyes. This was just what she had been hoping for all along.

Then, over the music, she suddenly heard loud noises. She opened her eyes and looked around.

Jake Hamilton and Denny Jacobson staggered into the living room, their hair speckled with frosting and their clothes stained with soda. Several of the other boys started laughing.

Out on the patio, someone screamed, "Food fight!"

Todd and Aaron quickly exchanged a look. Then they broke away from the twins and hurried to the refreshment table to arm themselves with cupcakes.

Elizabeth and Jessica stared after them in amazement. Suddenly, Jessica ducked as a melon ball came whizzing over her head. It missed Jessica by inches but struck Elizabeth squarely on the cheek.

"Hey!" Elizabeth protested.

The next thing she knew, Jake and Denny were pelting each other with heart-shaped mints, and Ken Matthews came barreling through the crowd, determined to drop a heart-shaped ice cube down the back of Patrick's shirt.

There was a shriek. "Look at my dress!" someone wailed.

"I don't believe it," Jessica said angrily.

Elizabeth shook her head. "What happened? It was all so romantic two seconds ago."

Amy appeared beside her and laughed. "I

guess I was right after all. The guys haven't changed a bit, have they?"

The twins began to laugh, too. "I guess they're not as mature as we thought," Elizabeth said ruefully.

"Let's get our stuff and go home," Amy said. "I think the party's over."

"Come spend the night at our house," Elizabeth suggested.

"Only if you promise not to talk about boys," Amy said with a laugh. "Deal?"

"Deal," Elizabeth said.

"Double deal," Jessica added.

The three girls shook hands on it.

They had just said good-bye to Ellen when Amy clutched Jessica's arm. "Look," she whispered. "It's Bruce and Veronica."

Bruce and Veronica were moving through the crowd in the living room toward the front door.

"It looks like they're leaving together," Elizabeth said in surprise. "Look! They're holding hands."

"Well!" Jessica said huffily. "He sure has a lot of nerve. He's supposed to be here with me."

"Jessica!" Amy and Elizabeth exclaimed simultaneously.

"Just kidding." Jessica grinned.

But as Bruce and Veronica passed by, Veronica turned and gave Jessica an ugly stare.

"Just a minute, Bruce," Jessica heard Veronica say in her most flirtatious voice. "I have to find my purse."

Veronica crossed over to where Jessica was standing and smiled sweetly. "Oh, Jessica," she cooed. "Could I talk to you for a minute?"

Jessica hesitated.

"It will only take a second," Veronica said coaxingly. "Come on." She motioned toward the hall.

"Go on," Elizabeth whispered. "Find out what she wants."

As soon as Jessica and Veronica were out of the others' sight, the sweet smile disappeared from Veronica's face. "I figured it out," she said in a nasty voice. "You were pretending to be Elizabeth, weren't you? That's how you knew about the locket."

Veronica reached up and tore the locket from her neck, breaking the chain. She dropped it contemptuously at Jessica's feet. "I owe you," she said threateningly. "And believe me, you'll get paid back."

Veronica pointed at Jessica, then drew her finger across her throat.

Jessica swallowed nervously and her eyes followed Veronica as she swept away. She knew that she didn't want Veronica for a friend. But she had a sinking feeling that she didn't want her for an enemy, either.

How will Veronica get her revenge? Find out in Sweet Valley Twins No 67, **JESSICA THE THIEF.**

We hope you enjoyed reading this book. If you would like to receive further information about available titles in the Bantam series, just write to the address below, with your name and address: Kim Prior, Bantam Books, 61–63 Uxbridge Road, Ealing, London W5 5SA.

If you live in Australia or New Zealand and would like more information about the series, please write to:

Sally Porter
Transworld Publishers
(Australia) Pty Ltd
15–25 Helles Avenue
Moorebank
NSW 2170
AUSTRALIA

Kiri Martin
Transworld Publishers (NZ) Ltd
3 William Pickering Drive
Albany
Auckland
NEW ZEALAND

All Bantam and Young Adult books are available at your bookshop or newsagent, or can be ordered from the following address: Corgi/Bantam Books, Cash Sales Department, PO Box 11, Falmouth, Cornwall, TR10 9EN.

Please list the title(s) you would like, and send together with a cheque or postal order to cover the cost of the book(s) plus postage and packing charges of £1.00 for one book, £1.50 for two books, and an additional 30p for each subsequent book ordered to a maximum of £3.00 for seven or more books.

(The above applies only to readers in the UK, and BFPO)

Overseas customers (including Eire), please allow £2.00 for postage and packing for the first book, an additional £1.00 for a second book, and 50p for each subsequent title ordered.